ANCIENT WISDOM

For centuries it has been known that in the heights of the Himalayas and hidden in secret Tibet there are Lamaseries with priceless manuscripts relating to the wisdom of the ancients. It is also believed that the MASTERS—the teachers or guides of those who seek enlightenment of the Soul—can be reached by those who need them.

These stories reveal to those who can understand a little of the esoteric knowledge perceived and closely guarded from the material world of the ignorant and cynical.

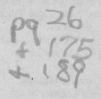

Bantam Books by Barbara Cartland
Ask your bookseller for the books you have missed

Barbara Cartland's Library of Love series

Barbara Cartland's Ancient Wisdom series

Barbara Cartland

The Forgotten City

A Novel of Ancient Wisdom

BANTAM BOOKS · TORONTO · NEW YORK · LONDON

THE FORGOTTEN CITY
A Bantam Book / August 1978

ISBN 0-553-12127-8

Published simultaneously in the United States and Canada

Bantam Books are published by Bantam Books, Inc. Its trade-
mark, consisting of the words "Bantam Books" and the por-
trayal of a bantam, is registered in the United States Patent
Office and in other countries. Marca Registrada. Bantam
Books, Inc., 666 Fifth Avenue, New York, New York 10019.

PRINTED IN THE UNITED STATES OF AMERICA

Introduction
by
Barbara Cartland

This book portrays a woman's pilgrimage as she searches, at first blindly, for the enlightenment and illumination of her mind and her soul.

I have tried to show that there is something to be learnt from every contact we make with other people, from every difficulty, from every disillusionment. Only in finding the Spiritual love which is part of the Divine can we find ourselves.

THE WISDOM OF ASIA

There is a road, steep and thorny, beset with perils of every kind—but yet a road; and it leads to the Heart of the Universe. I can tell you how to find Those who will show you the secret gateway that leads inward only, and closes fast behind the neophyte forevermore.

There is no danger that dauntless courage cannot conquer. There is no trial that spotless purity cannot pass through. There is no difficulty that strong intellect cannot surmount.

For those who win onwards, there is reward past all telling: the power to bless and save humanity. For those who fail, there are other lives in which success may come.

—*H. P. Blavatsky*

Chapter One

1935

The trees in the Great Park were dark silhouettes against the sky and high over the house climbed the first star.

In the dining-room, on the polished, silver-laden table tall candles gleamed through parchment shades.

Sir Henry Brantfield rose slowly from his chair as the silently moving parlour-maids placed a large dish on the serving-table and stood aside, waiting for him to perform his usual ritual of carving.

"These are fine fat ducks, Mother," he said to his wife.

"They are from the home farm, dear," she answered.

With a chuckle Sir Henry turned to their guest.

"You won't get better than these at the Ritz," he said jovially. "There is nothing like home-grown stuff; very little comes into this dining-room that is not our own."

Pamela did not answer, although the remark was addressed to her.

There was no need, for Sir Henry's back was towards her as he carved—and besides, she had received identical information at every meal at which she had taken part at Cowton Hall.

It was Sir Henry's invariable question, to which

1

Lady Brantfield replied automatically with the same words and the same gentle smile, as though she were an actress playing a familiar rôle.

Even when husband and wife were alone, Pamela felt that the same tradition was maintained. She knew that when they were with their son he took the part of guest, which was now hers.

Arthur, it seemed to her, was a stranger now that she saw him in his own home.

The Arthur of Cowton Hall was in no way the man whom Pamela had known in her own home; the friend who had held her father's affection; the companion with whom she had found so much in common during the past six months.

Looking at him across the dining-room table, over the large bowl of pink carnations grown in Sir Henry's glass-houses, she was conscious for the first time that he looked a middle-aged man.

It was not the faint showing of grey hairs round his temples or the thinness of the hair on the top of his head; it was something more subtle—a lack of vitality.

The pseudo-Jacobean panelling put in by Sir Henry, which decorated the dining-room, was as alien to the walls of the old house as were the Brantfields themselves.

For nearly three hundred years Cowton Hall had belonged to the family who had built it.

In the Boer War the Cowtons of that time lost their only son. A year later, the last of the family was carried down the broad oak staircase and taken to the family vault in the little Church-yard a quarter of a mile from the house.

It was then that Mr. Henry Brantfield, inheritor himself of a prosperous business, decided that he would move into the country.

At first his wife withstood his persuasions; she was afraid of this great, stately house, which seemed to her too large and far too disdainful ever to become a home.

Overruled by her husband's ambition, and born of a generation when women acquiesced rather than argued, she shed bitter tears as she packed in the Villa which for five years of happily married life had been her pride.

Cowton Hall neither received nor rebutted the intruders; it treated them as interlopers, disdainful of their existence.

Lady Brantfield had always felt slightly apologetic for her presence. She still walked softly in the high picture-gallery and on the polished floor of the large white drawing-room, as if she hoped by such gentleness to be overlooked.

Perhaps the atmosphere which she sensed was in some way responsible for the boasting joviality of her husband, which as years went by grew into almost a defiance.

"Dammit!" he seemed to say to the house. "I'm paying. At least show a friendly gratitude towards me."

Even their furniture appeared alien. The Cowton relatives had taken most of the heirlooms. Sir Henry had tried to buy the house "lock, stock, and barrel"—his own words—but they had refused.

London decorators had been engaged and had been given carte blanche. They did their best, but the house would have none of them.

From the walls the Cowton family had taken all the great gilt-framed portraits. Portraits of the Brantfields were hung instead.

Over the carving-table was one of Mr. George Brantfield, the founder and inventor of Brantfield's Paper Bags, Limited.

He had a fine face, and there was character in the steady eyes and the firm mouth above the short grey beard. He was an honest man, too, with no pretensions.

The picture of Sir Henry had been commissioned to one of London's leading artists shortly after he had obtained his title from the Lloyd George Government.

It was the picture of a prosperous businessman trying a little too hard to forget his business.

It was like Sir Henry himself: there was the same jovial smile without humour, the anxiety to please, and the ambition to attain, but there was no character in the face.

The picture was that of a pompous man intent only on obtaining good value for his thousand guineas.

Opposite where Pamela was sitting, and behind Arthur, so that it stood over him like some symbolic tableau of progression, was a picture of Arthur when he was a boy.

It was extraordinarily badly painted and showed a fat, stupid-looking child, holding a large dog by the collar, staring full-face at the artist in spiritless obedience.

Pamela hated the picture. She felt that it was this which had first begun to show her in a different light the man she had promised to marry.

The Arthur she knew was interesting, clever in a companionable way, sympathetic and understanding, and someone whom her father had found congenial.

It was a revolutionary thought for her to wonder if perhaps Arthur's congeniality had been that he was a good listener.

Had he indeed played no part save an inferior one in what she had imagined to be a stimulating and equal friendship in spite of the disparity in age?

When her father had come to London, accepting, on her mother's insistence, the position at London University, it had been Arthur who had dragged him from his despondency, depression, and loneliness.

He had introduced interesting men to the house and insisted that her father should receive their hospitality in return.

Because of this, Pamela had always thought of him as someone whose opinion she was proud to seek and glad to accept. Now she doubted it.

Here at Cowton Hall, Arthur was swamped into lethargy. It was like being smothered with cotton-wool, deafened and blinded by it.

She had a wild desire to scream, to beat her hands on the table, yet she felt with the impotent helplessness of a nightmare that nothing she did would make an impression, nothing could alter that stifling atmosphere.

Here in the dining-room they sat like people who were not alive, or who existed only in a dream.

They appeared to be acting over and over again some dull play, doing what they did only for the sake of an audience, having no personal existence outside the rôles they had assumed.

Pamela tried to argue herself out of her own conviction, but throughout the week that she had stayed at Cowton Hall, every day had brought clearer to her mind the impossibility of her even trying to like Sir Henry and Lady Brantfield.

Arthur had not spoken of them very often in the past.

He had referred occasionally to his home, but casually, without giving her the impression that it meant anything more than the place where his father and mother lived.

There was not the glow and the swift emotion

which Pamela had grown to associate with the word.

Home to her meant that grey stone house behind which the purple moors rose, and to which her thoughts returned so often that it was as though she had never left it.

There had always been Tarns at Glenferry. Every nook and corner of Glenferry had a joy, an interest, and a familiarity.

What did the lack of paint on the lintels matter when the sun came shining in through the windows as if it were glad to be there?

And the wind blew a welcome through the broken shutters, and there was laughter in the sound of the wallpaper crackling where it was torn away from the wall in the sitting-room.

There was a warmth in the smoky peat fires which no amount of central heating or well-laid coal could give at Cowton Hall.

Pamela thought of it now, lonely and empty save for the old keeper's wife who was caretaking, though her job was a sinecure, for there was little enough of which to take care.

One day her brother Ion would go back there, perhaps one day he would make money enough to be rich and famous, but he would go home.

Glenferry was in his blood as it had been in her father's.

Mechanically Pamela helped herself to the savoury. She agreed with some trivial remark of Sir Henry's and met Arthur's eyes across the table with a polite smile. There was no conversational effort required at Cowton Hall, for Sir Henry kept up a flow of small-talk.

"My green-houses are the best in the county," he said to Pamela.

Although she had no way of knowing whether they were or not, she agreed with him because it was so obviously expected of her.

Sir Henry raised his glass to Pamela.

"Your health, my daughter-in-law-to-be," he said. "Arthur, you will join me in drinking to your lady, who will one day be the chatelaine at Cowton."

"Chatelaine at Cowton"!

Pamela felt herself shiver at the words. Sir Henry had a habit of giving people titles; he enjoyed doing that almost as much as he enjoyed the possession of his own.

She forced herself to say a few words and to smile in response to the raised glasses of the two men.

'I can't do it!' she thought to herself. 'I can't bear a lifetime of this.'

* * *

Lady Brantfield seated herself in the corner of the sofa in the library. The large drawing-room was used only when there were guests.

She was making a muffler for the Personal Service League, but when Pamela had offered to help she had seemed surprised at the suggestion.

"Surely you have work of your own to do, dear," she said gently. "I know what a lot of things one requires for a trousseau."

"I am not a very good needlewoman," Pamela had confessed guiltily.

Having counted her stitches this evening, Lady Brantfield said:

"I had a letter from your mother this morning."

"From Mother?" Pamela questioned in surprise.

"It was in answer to mine," came the reply. "I wrote to her several days ago. It was a secret, but now that it is all decided, I can tell you what it is about, although it was my husband's idea and not mine, so you must thank him."

"Thank him for what?" Pamela asked, slightly bewildered.

"We thought, and Arthur agreed," Lady Brantfield went on, "that it would be so nice if you were married from here, the Church being in the grounds, and the tenants would like to take part in the celebrations.

"Of course we know that your mother is not well off, and it would be a relief to her if she could leave all the arrangements in our hands.

"Naturally we did not say anything until it was fixed up, in case you would be disappointed, but I told Arthur this evening before dinner and he was delighted."

"But I hadn't thought of it . . . I mean to say, what has Mother arranged?" Pamela asked, stumbling over her words as she found difficulty in choosing them.

"Your mother agrees with me," Lady Brantfield said, "that it will be best for her and your sister and brothers to come and stay here."

She lowered her voice as she went on.

"I know that you wish for quite a quiet wedding, as it is not yet a year since your father's death, but of course if there is anyone you particularly want to ask, I am sure we can arrange it."

Almost without thinking what she was doing, Pamela rose to her feet and moved across the room. She did not know why the idea of being married at Cowton should fill her with such dismay.

She knew that her mother would be only too delighted to save the expense and that Lady Brantfield's suggestion would have been received with acclamation.

Pamela was not surprised by her mother's extreme gratification at Arthur's proposal of marriage; in fact she expected it.

She knew that for a long time Mrs. Tarn had been hoping that her eldest daughter would be married before the second left school. Jean was her favourite child, and the boys, Andrew and Jock, held a place in her affections unattained by her eldest son.

Ion and Pamela were, in the words of the old saying, "their father's children," and Mrs. Tarn not only gave them little understanding but wasted little interest in them.

Of Welsh descent, she had an extraordinary hardness where her affections were not concerned.

For those she loved she would scheme, plan, and sacrifice herself without stint, but she had no superficial generosity or even affection for the two children of her bearing who had seemed alien to her from their birth.

Coming from a large, noisy family, she had been miserably lonely at Glenferry when she first married.

Her husband, immersed in the estate, his books, and his sports, had found little time to discover that the surface brightness of his young wife's manner hid a shrinking, frightened, and rather unhappy child.

Elizabeth Tarn took her time growing up. She developed into an efficient and self-sufficient person, but in the meantime Ion, her eldest child, and Pamela, had been born.

Andrew and Jock had followed later, and they too were but echoes of their mother's strong personality. There was little of the Tarn in either of them, their characteristics all Welsh.

Ion was the strangest of the family. He had his father's looks and a quick, vivid brain. As a small boy he was moody and restless, liable to forget time,

meals, or even nightfall if he was puzzling something
out for himself.

The lights on the hills, the sudden flight of the
grouse over the heather, a heron wending its way up
the river, or the flash of salmon in the falls would
bring him, as it were, to life.

He would glow with the beauty of it, often shout-
ing incoherently, or standing rigidly still as if the
whole of his being went out to what he saw, and he
had no thought, conscious or unconscious, for the
movement of his body.

His father's brain was scientific and critical,
which showed first in his earlier works and later at
London University, where it made him one of the
greatest teachers of metaphysics who had ever held
a lecture-room breathless.

He taught the children at Glenferry, and Ion
would listen, knitting his dark eye-brows, seemingly
detached until suddenly some word or phrase would
light him up in radiance.

"I see it! I understand!" he would cry, and words
would tumble out of his mouth in his efforts to explain
and capture his own thoughts.

Pamela, four years younger, would sit, even
when quite a child, fascinated by her father's teaching. He would make things live for her more easily
and more often than he could for Ion.

Yet, in her comprehension she never reached the
heights or achieved the vision of her brother, but remained balanced, limited, though progressing steadily towards the knowledge her father tried to give her.

They worked hard in the untidy, rather dingy
gun-room which served as a school-room in the morn-
ings because in it there was a large, strong table at
which all three could sit at once.

There was no place for children in their father's own room, where he wrote far into the night at the articles and books which brought him fame but little money.

Pamela could remember her mother reading the appreciations of some new work, proud of her husband and saying so in a half-grudging, half-elated way, while at the back door the local grocer refused to leave his goods unless he was paid for them.

Looking back, she realised how poor they had been at Glenferry, but to her those years were so happy that she found it difficult to recall the scantiness of the meals, the discomforts of the house, and the thinness of her own clothing.

It was not until 1928 that her father understood how he had been able to live in his home.

In the slump, when Welsh coal-mines were closed, never to open again, colliers lost their livelihood and many hundreds of people lost their savings and their income.

The Laird of Glenferry was faced with the facts that his wife's small income had ceased to exist, her capital was exhausted, and in the future he himself must be the breadwinner of the household.

His work the year before had brought him unstinted praise from every International Authority and the sum of fifty pounds in cash.

There were five children to feed, and himself and his wife, but while he waited, wondering helplessly about the future, Mrs. Tarn was busy.

Without her husband's knowledge, she wrote to a number of his most distinguished admirers in London. A week later came the offer of a post at London University, with a salary of six hundred pounds a year.

At first her husband refused to accept. To leave Glenferry was to him the equivalent of committing suicide.

He had lived there all his life, and his family had lived there since the early days of Scotland's history. If his wife liked, he would let the moors, cut down expenses—as though Elizabeth might then have had any to be cut down—but to uproot himself was impossible.

For the first and only time in her life Pamela saw her father angry.

He roared a refusal and rushed out of the dining-room, where the letter had been read, slamming the none-too-secure door so that the whole room jumped and vibrated with his wrath.

For a whole day he was lost in the hills, and when he returned he was in a very different mood. He listened to his wife's arguments, knowing in his heart that he had already accepted them.

The moors were barren, there was nothing to let, and if they lowered their expenses they would starve. There were seven mouths to feed, and the only asset of the estate was peat and they could not live on that.

A month later they left, travelling south in the express, a silent party, three of whom felt that the end of the world had come upon them.

Her father never recovered. He was like a plant which was uprooted too late to make a fresh start.

He hated the small, meagre little house in Kensington where they lived too closely to one another.

He hated London, with its roar of traffic, its stifling, airless streets, the confinement of conventional clothes, and the atmosphere of respectability into which his job plunged him.

Even his work suffered, because he could not throw down his pen and take his pupils and himself for a tramp over the moors to clear their brains and to find in the silence and the succour of nature the answers to their questions.

Two weeks after the Tarns had settled in London, Ion left home. He walked out of the house without a farewell to any member of the family.

Only his father seemed unsurprised, as though something he may have said had prepared him, or perhaps it was just sympathy with his son that gave him understanding.

Pamela thought at first that Ion would go back to Glenferry. She herself would have slept on the floor there and lived on scraps, could she have dared it.

How Ion lived in the years that followed, what he did and where he went, was to remain a mystery. It was two years later that a book of his was published and he sent a copy to his father.

Had he not done so, it was doubtful whether any of them would have been aware of its existence. It was only a very slim book of poems, and while the few notices it received were encouraging, the general public remained ignorant of its birth.

The poems were immature but undoubtedly they held promise, and Pamela remembered her father poring over them, reading them again and again, occasionally quoting a line or two, trying not to criticise so much as to understand what the author had meant, what was the thought behind his creation.

A year or so later another book appeared, and that was followed by a third.

All this time they had no news of Ion.

From the poems, they learnt that he had been

in Florence, had visited Greece, and had been influenced by the battlefields of France and the rivers of Germany.

Only when their father died did he send, surprisingly, a cheque for twenty-five pounds, commanding that his father's body should be taken to Glenferry and buried there.

He wrote from France and gave his address, and Pamela felt that her mother would have defied his instructions had she not been afraid that, as head of the family, he would come home and insist on his orders being obeyed.

And so to Glenferry, to home, the Laird went for the last time, and it was with bitterness in her heart that Pamela knew they could afford only one mourner to go north, and that inevitably must be her mother.

Money difficulties indeed had seemed to increase rather than diminish with the years. Both the boys were at public schools and her sister, Jean, was specialising in secretarial work, all of which entailed further expense.

Pamela herself tried various small jobs in London, but while her father had been alive she had found that there was endless work to be done at home.

The house, small as it was, could not be managed entirely by her mother, even with the help of a charwoman who came in daily to do the scrubbing.

Pamela disliked domesticity, but there was no other course open to her. She had neither the influence nor the technique nor the training for any kind of business post.

While her father was alive, her duties were less irksome in that she found happiness in doing even the smallest things for him, although he never noticed that his socks were well darned or that his study was better kept than any other room in the house.

As the years passed, Pamela's affection for her father grew into something so deep and fundamentally part of herself that when he died she was like some semi-paralysed creature or a person who had suddenly, without warning, lost an arm or a leg.

She moved mechanically, as it were, about her household duties, greeting her little world with a calmness which surprised them, while all the time her mind and emotions were numbed with shock.

Indeed, her grief was more like that of a beloved wife after years of happiness than that of a child for a parent.

It was Arthur, more than anyone else, who realised how overwhelming Pamela's misery was, and he had done his best, in his quiet, friendly way, to help her through the first terrible months.

Years of hardship and struggle had brought to Mrs. Tarn a resilience which stood her in good stead in her widowhood.

She had loved her husband, but loved him with the same maternal affection that she had given to her three younger children, and the tears she shed for him were those of a mother.

But to Pamela it was as if the rock on which she leant, or the foundation on which she was built, had given way.

Arthur arrived not suddenly or tremendously into her life, as in some fictitious romance, but so calmly that it was as if he had always been there.

Indeed, her mother's joy and delight at the thought of the marriage was far more emotional than her own calm acceptance of Arthur's proposal.

Yet, while she was content to become engaged and to think of the future as comfortable and secure in Arthur's guardianship, she inexplicably shrank from the actual ceremony.

There was, she knew, no reasonable excuse for delay; indeed, from the family's point of view, the more speedy the marriage the more sensible it would be.

One less mouth to feed, one item less for Mrs. Tarn to consider in her budget.

Pamela had come to Cowton for a week, and she had known that while visiting Arthur's parents it was to be expected that they would fix the actual date of the ceremony.

Yet, Lady Brantfield's suggestion of her being married there, and the announcement of her mother's acceptance, quite unreasonably scared Pamela into chaotic thought and indecision.

Before she could answer or express her feelings to Lady Brantfield, the door opened and Arthur and his father came into the room.

With a sensitiveness which was noticeable only where Pamela was concerned, Arthur saw that something was wrong.

While he kept the conversation on general lines, his eyes continually sought Pamela's face.

Earlier than usual she rose and asked if she might go to bed.

He followed her into the hall.

"There is nothing you want?" he asked gently, lowering his voice, for the library door was left open behind him.

"Nothing," Pamela replied, her hand on the bannister.

"You are quite sure?" Arthur insisted.

He was striving to put into the words his own uneasiness that something was amiss, and yet he felt tongue-tied and ineffective.

"Nothing, thank you," Pamela answered again. "Good-night, Arthur."

Slowly, not looking back, she went up the broad stairway, while he, with a faint frown, stood silently watching her.

* * *

In her own bed-room, Pamela closed the door behind her, then stood for a moment with her hand on the door-knob.

Across the room she was reflected in a big mahogany-framed mirror, but she did not see herself.

Her eyes stared straight ahead, yet she was looking inwards, as people do when they search themselves or their conscience for something more hard to discover than any superficial disturbance.

Slowly Pamela undressed, moving with the deliberation of someone who gives no thought to what he does but performs each movement from habit.

Only as she turned out the lights by the dressing-table, leaving on just the one shaded lamp by the bed-side, did her face lighten with an eager expression as her glance rested on the book which lay beside her bed.

In its blue paper wrapper, Arthur had given it to her a few hours ago, and her heart had leapt at the name of the author, inscribed in old English lettering below the title, *The Forgotten City*.

On their journey up to Cowton, Arthur had suddenly remarked:

"I see your brother has brought out another book."

"When? Where? What is it?" Pamela had asked.

She was conscious that underlying her interest was also a strange disappointment that Ion had not sent her a copy.

Not that during the past years he had noticed her existence any more than he had noticed that of the rest of the family. It was to his father that he had sent his works, enclosing neither a letter nor any other information about himself.

But Pamela knew that her father had written in return, and she believed that the sympathy between them was unbroken even with the years of their separation.

For her own part, she loved Ion and believed in him as completely today as she had when they had been companions on the moors of Glenferry.

Arthur's newspaper had told her that Ion's new book was a success.

Already the critics were beginning to speak of his poems as a contribution to English literature, and already they welcomed any work of his, praising unstintingly his last book, which had been a translation from the Latin.

This new work, *The Forgotten City*, was, Pamela learnt, a long poem, and his most ambitious achievement so far.

"Oh, I must get it," she said to Arthur.

"I will write tonight," he said, smiling at her, "as soon as we arrive."

"You don't think we could buy it at the next town?" she had questioned; but he had shaken his head.

"It has only been out two or three days," he had said, "and I don't think it is the sort of book people buy casually. I will get it for you as quickly as possible."

.But it had taken several days, and only by that afternoon's post had come the brown cardboard parcel for which Pamela had waited so eagerly.

She had not allowed herself to glance inside it

while she was dressing for dinner, because she wanted time and quiet; now, slipping between the linen sheets and propping the pillows up behind her, she opened it slowly.

Reading his name—*Ion Tarn*—on the title-page, a swift vision of him came to her.

It had been a cold, crisp spring morning at Glenferry, and they had crept from the house before breakfast, finding in the keen, clear air a promise of adventure and excitement to which every nerve in their small bodies responded.

There was a light on the moors, a mist on the hill-tops, and that sense of being part of sky, sea, and hills which comes so unconsciously to children and so miraculously to older people.

They had walked in silence down the hillside to the river, the morning wind whipping the colour into their cheeks and blowing Ion's dark hair in untidy wisps over his wide forehead.

His eyes were dark and sombre as they often were when he was thinking deeply, his lower lip thrust forward a little, while his long arms swinging in his outgrown and shrunken sweater seemed to beat time to some rhythm within himself.

Pamela was conscious of a happiness and harmony between them which made her steps light and dancing as she moved beside her brother.

She knew that it was a day of enjoyment which comes only to those who live by intuition rather than reason, and it seemed to her that their whole life might begin and end in the wonder of this spring morning.

They came to the falls, the silvery water falling, shimmering its way round and over the dark rocks, the noise of it heady, intoxicating, turbulent, and yet it was a music they could both understand.

As they watched, a great cock-salmon came swimming up the river. Two untidy, carelessly dressed children in outgrown clothes, they were filled with a sudden exaltation, a kind of wild triumph of happiness and delight.

He jumped, a flash of curved silver, fell back, and tried again. They held their breath . . . he was over.

Then Ion went mad. With a strange cry, he ran, jumping and leaping, over the slippery wet rocks which bordered the falls.

"I am a salmon! I am he who wins the falls!" he cried, his words winging their way back to Pamela above the roar of the water.

She watched him, her heart in her mouth, feeling that every moment he must fall and slip into the torrent.

There was a strange grace, a wildness, and a beauty in his white face and his waving hair as he danced and ran on the very edge of the falling water, and she seemed to see in him a resemblance to the great fish which had conquered the falls and had now gone on up the river.

Boy and fish, in her mind they were one, both creatures with a strange, wild beauty, both in some way part of each other, and even while she stood outside she could understand.

She had waited, afraid and yet curiously glad. Ion had not fallen, and in a little while he had come back to her, slipping his hand into hers. It had been damp with spray, yet burningly hot, as if his very life were pulsing through his fingertips.

Slowly they had moved on towards the sea, never at any time referring to what had passed, yet completely in sympathy one with the other. . . .

The vision passed. Pamela turned to the next

page and found a short note signed by the author, which said:

> In writing of the "Forgotten City" I have followed closely to a legend which is still repeated round the firesides of Northern Italy. So far as I can discover, no story-teller has attempted to put on paper this tale which yet finds some credulous folk who believe in it.

Pamela smiled. It was an abrupt prelude but she understood Ion's attitude.

There was some honesty which made him take no credit for the tale itself and some defiance which made him add that his treatment owed nothing to other authors.

She seemed to see the line of his jaw, square-set, and the lowering of his dark eye-brows which was so characteristic of him in argument, and then eagerly she turned to the first page.

The poem began:

> 'Twas summer, and the honeyladen bees
> Hummed from the tall annunciation flowers
> Which held in Gabriel's hand
> First came to earth
> To visit her, whose purity and faith
> Could find no equal in the House of God,
> And so became in very truth a Home
> For God Himself.
> Pale symbol of that beauty
> Lilies stood
> Yielding their fragrant treasure to the thieves. . . .

The following lines swiftly described the peace and healing of the Monastery garden, the dark purple shadows beneath arched cloisters, the calm serenity of the stone walls mellowed by the weather of centuries, and the paths worn smooth by sandalled feet.

There were beds for herbs used for bodily ills and those set aside for the growing of vegetables.

There were green lawns stretching down to the orchards, the fruit ripening on the trees, the deep river flowing swiftly by, and the sunlight glittering on the water and throwing through the cool, dark leaves of overhanging trees a dappled pattern of gold on grassy banks.

One felt the beauty of the English countryside, and listened to the murmur of voices rising from the Chapel and the slow footsteps of monks moving in contemplation along the stone corridors.

Outside in the world there were troubles, the Church still fighting for security, for power, and for justice, but here there were men giving their lives to the service of God.

The poem went on:

> *Only the music of the bees,*
> *And the sweet scent of blossoming flowers,*
> *Crept through the lattice windows of a cell,*
> *Where knelt the Abbot John in anguished prayer.*

Instantly a new note was struck. The calm peace was broken. "Anguish"—the emotion vibrated across the pages, creating disharmony, bringing a question in its train.

Pamela read on:

The last Abbot of the Monastery had died. He had appointed as his successor a young man, a disciple he loved, one who had in everything shown himself worthy of the high position to which he was now called.

Yet even as the Abbot John had taken over his

duties, even as he had bowed to the responsibility and to the knowledge that his whole life must be one of service to those men who looked to him as leader, a call had come to him from outside.

The peace he had found in perfect obedience was disturbed.

Surely and certainly the Abbot John knew that he must make a pilgrimage to Rome to ask the blessing of the Father of the Church, the Pope.

The monks would have dissuaded him, saying that these were no times to venture abroad. He himself agreed with them, and wished to stay, yet stronger than any argument was the command within him to depart.

> *Where reason bade him stay*
> *Instinct of heart and mind bade him set forth.*
> *Some power within himself,*
> *Beyond emotion, faith, or Love of God,*
> *Compelled him to obey;*
> *And set a pilgrim's staff*
> *Within his hand.*

After many farewells the Abbot left, setting forth into the world dressed as a travelling Friar, with no servant save the humility of his mind, no protector save his courage and his staff.

A fair wind took him across the Channel, but on foreign soil troubles came. Adventures of all kinds tempted and tried him; but, his faith steadfast, his determination unswerving, he travelled on towards Rome.

Then, as he neared the Alps, he met a cavalcade richly arrayed.

A lady who travels also to obtain the blessing of God's representative on earth asks his assistance.

Donna Christina was born of a high Spanish family, an heiress to vast estates.

Her hand is sought in marriage by two suitors, and, partly to prolong their wooing and partly because she is a devout daughter of the Church, she has determined before her marriage to make a pilgrimage to Rome.

On the journey her Priest and confessor dies, and as her party overtakes the Abbot John, she sends her servants to beg him to hear their confessions and to administer to them the Holy Sacrament.

He grants her request, but in their meeting a strange and amazing exaltation seizes them both.

It is as if they recognise each other, and every moment they spend together seems to create in both of them such a closeness of sympathy that it is as if in some forgotten past they had been much—nay, all—to each other.

Fighting in shame what seems to him to be a desperate temptation, the Abbot John is gradually drawn nearer and nearer to a confession of his love.

Finally they arrive at a little Italian town high among the Alps. The party spend the night there among the snowy mountain-peaks, far away from the world and civilisation.

Their consciences, doubts, and everything save love is lost in the same mist which obscures the land below them.

Through the torture of his despair in what he believes is a desecration of his office and his vows to God, he is upheld by a strange power which tells him that this transcending love is beyond all ties or bonds—that it is inevitable, and that this woman and he are part of each other for all time.

In a long and very beautiful passage, the Abbot moves slowly towards his lady's room, every step seeming to demand the sacrifice of some part of himself, the crucifixion of that pride which believed that his faith and creed were greater than this miracle of love.

Only by complete forgetfulness of self, by complete abandonment of everything but the absolute truth, can man face the perfection of love.

And so the Abbot comes slowly to the woman who awaits him. He speaks:

> *"In dying are we born,*
> *And if some part on this pale earth*
> *Must fade because I hold you in my arms,*
> *Why then I would embrace the cross itself*
> *If through the sacrifice of self be found*
> *The glory of a love which must be God's."*

Donna Christina knows too that this is the moment for which she has waited not only in this brief life but through all eternity.

The moment has come; it is meant that they should be submerged one in the other, and that no bonds made by man, even though forged by his faith in God, can stand against love.

From the moment of their meeting she has recognised in this tall, fair, ascetic Englishman something which seems as familiar to her as her own self.

As in love, each is but a reflection of the other, and she sees mirrored in the Abbot John all the beauty that she has ever sought within herself, and she knows that. . . .

> *She too had known in some forgotten life*
> *This man, his love, this sacrament of self,*
> *And memories' resurrection came. . . .*

Pamela put down the book for a moment.
She had read for nearly two hours, completely

unconscious of herself, of her surroundings, of everything except the story unfolding before her eyes.

Yet now it seemed to her as if behind the story, or rather within it, deeper than the tale and stronger than the superficial emotion it aroused, there was a message.

It almost escaped her; it remained tantalisingly unexpressed, yet it sought expression.

This idea had been growing within her as she read, and now the words "memories' resurrection" seemed to stimulate her mind until she forced it to find and express the inspirations which flew like winged birds from the burden of the words.

Is there a Forgotten City, she asked herself, within everyone?

That progression which each individual seeks—was it to be found not, as was believed, in the future, but in the past; within, not without?

So that for happiness, peace, inspiration, and faith, one should look back and not forward, seeking a resurrection, if the knowledge of God within us is not to be acquired but rediscovered?

She re-turned the pages of the book, reading again the passages where the Abbot John and Donna Christina recognise each other and, as it were, renew their love.

Then she went on and finished the book.

She found that the story ended with the consummation of a love far beyond any earthly joy, its completeness and its beauty absolving the Abbot from his vows and showing that even the service of God must be laid aside when God Himself is revealed in perfect love.

An earthquake shakes the mountain on which is built the little City in which they are staying, a volcanic eruption hides the path to Rome and isolates from the eyes of men the lovers and those who serve them.

The end of the story was deliberately unfinished.

One might believe that even today the City remains impregnable, yet intact, holding the living descendents of that great romance.

Or one could think that God showed His wrath —a just punishment for those who disobeyed Him by the quenching and destruction of their lives.

There came the question: "Could such love be destroyed?" Was it not living, even in the legend?

Living because two people had manifested that which was absolute, complete, a perfection which in itself could never die.

Having finished the story, Pamela lay back on her pillows, with closed eyes. She was not tired, in fact she had never felt more animated, more fresh with vitality.

It was as though every word had stimulated and revivified her. Again and again the words "memories' resurrection" came whispering in her ears, and each time they seemed to clear the chaos of her thoughts.

The inertia and the languor of the past months disappeared.

Further back still, it swept away the years she had spent in London, attuning herself to the noise and bustle, to the education of everyday life, to the weariness of domesticity.

Breaking through, gloriously resurrected, came the ardent sincerity of pulsating youth, came the knowledge which had been hers in childhood, of that freedom of spirit which knows no horizons and acknowledges no boundaries.

After a time she sat up in bed, placing her hands on her burning cheeks, her eyes shining, her mouth trembling.

Ion's book had awakened her. She was like a woman who responds to the passion of a lover, like a martyr who understands the true ecstasy of death and welcomes it with open arms.

For a long, long time she sat there. Slowly the colour and the beauty gave place to reason.

Pamela saw again the familiar outlines of her bed-room, but even as the confines of time and place enclosed her, she knew that she had found again her freedom and had returned to the City within herself.

WISDOM FROM THE EARLY CHURCH FATHERS

This world is not the only world. Every soul has existed from the beginning: it has therefore passed through some worlds already and will pass through others before it reaches the final consummation.

It comes into this world strengthened by the victories or weathered by the defeats of its previous life.

Its place in the world as a vessel appointed to honour or dishonour is determined by its previous merits or demerits. Its work in this world determines its place in the world which is to follow this.

—Origen

Chapter Two

⬛■━━━━━━■━━━━■━━━━■━━━━■━━━━■━━━━■━

O ften the most important decisions in life are made calmly and with a serenity which surprises only when on looking back we see how vital that time was, how important that particular decision.

Pamela, driving south in Arthur's grey two-seater, felt none of the agitation which might have been expected of her at such a moment.

The depth of her feelings could not show itself superficially by any of the flutterings or fretful nervousness with which men and women far too often cloud main issues.

All through the dark hours of the night she had read and reread parts of Ion's book, putting it down every now and then to savour, as it were, the full force of her own reactions to his words.

Occasionally she dozed a little until her thoughts mingled with dreams, her spirit still uplifted into realms too free of happiness for any formulated expression.

As the dawn broke and the first glimmer of pale light crept through the curtained windows, Pamela rose and dressed.

Her suitcase had fortunately been placed in the dressing-room which adjoined her bed-room; without haste she packed, and when ready she walked down the broad staircase to the hall door.

Only as she undid the chain and turned the big iron key did she hesitate and turn aside into the library, pulling back the curtains to let in the morning light. At the writing-desk she paused, and taking a sheet of paper wrote rapidly with a pencil:

> *Dear Arthur,*
> *I am going to find Ion. I must. I can't marry you. I am sorry.*
> > *Pamela.*
>
> *P.S.: I have taken the car. I will let you know where I leave it. Please don't try to stop me.*

She added the last words as an afterthought, thinking that Arthur might conceivably try to reach Southampton before her.

She was, however, not really afraid of his intervention, for she had faith in Arthur's good sense where she herself was concerned.

In spite of his conventionality, Arthur had a strange understanding of other people's vagaries. If any of his friends had suddenly announced his intention of leaving for Timbuctoo to marry a Hottentot, he would never have questioned his decision.

That this sudden departure of hers would affect him personally, to a degree that might, for once, upset the balance of his understanding, was not the reason that she added her postscript.

It was because in the days she had spent at Cowton she had become increasingly aware of the difference between Arthur and his parents.

Sir Henry was the type of person who always arrived at a railway station at least half-an-hour before the train was signalled, who never travelled unless his seat was engaged and his tickets were booked by a reliable agency.

Pamela could imagine that leaving England at a moment's notice would seem to him almost crazy in its imprudency, apart from the fact that without explanation or excuse she was refusing to marry his son.

Arthur, spurred on by his parents, might follow her; it was unlikely, but possible. Such a contingency, however, was worth only a moment's thought; it caused her no anxiety.

It did not seem to Pamela as though she were running away, in the real sense of escaping.

This was no more than the quiet arrival of a moment when she must go, and the doors to freedom were open, showing her a new path, which she must approach unencumbered.

It was not even surprising that she had a passport. Arthur had procured one for her only a fortnight ago when they had been talking, or rather he had, of a honeymoon abroad, and Pamela had mentioned quite casually the fact that she had never had a passport.

With his usual methodical care, Arthur had obtained one at once and she had accepted it, carelessly slipping it into the inner pocket of the bag she usually carried, where it had remained ever since.

As when the gods provide for us they provide generously, it was to be expected that Pamela should at this moment also have quite a large amount of money with her.

She had been intending to buy herself several new dresses but had not found what she wanted.

It was a misty morning and the dust from the wheels rose in a cloud behind her, covering the hedgerows and powdering the pink and white dog-roses, which were in full bloom.

Pamela did not hurry—the boat for St. Malo did not leave until the evening, and she had plenty of time to cover the two hundred miles between her and Southampton.

It was over six months since Ion had written from Bugalé, in Brittany, on her father's death, and yet she had no fear but that she would find him there, or at the next place to which he had gone.

How many years had passed since she had last seen him only surprised her when she thought of it.

He seemed so close to her now, so much part of herself that she could not believe that such a length of time had passed by without their meeting or exchanging a word.

Yet she knew that letters or communications are meaningless between two people who really matter to each other.

Ion and she had never needed words, for they moved to the same rhythm, their bodies in harmony as had been their minds and thoughts.

When Ion had left home, Pamela had taken his departure with a calmness which had surprised both her father and her mother, because although she had missed him physically, mentally she had known herself to be still in tune with him.

Ion could never have thrived in the close, commonplace atmosphere of the Kensington home. The confines which such a life involved were utterly alien to him.

In Glenferry he would often disappear for twenty-four hours on end, walking away over the moors, to return physically tired and ready for sleep and food, but with his eyes glowing, his whole being vibrating as from some tremendous stimulus.

In London, Ion could not have found solitude, nor could he have borne the veneer of respectability and conventionality which was gradually introduced to mellow and tame the Tarn family to their new surroundings.

Elizabeth Tarn had never really renounced the strong religious upbringing of her childhood and all the discipline which went with it.

But she had been infatuated enough with her husband, when his love-making had swept her off her feet and into the wilds of Scotland, to adapt herself to the happy-go-lucky atmosphere at Glenferry.

The neighbours, the servants, and anyone who happened to be passing would drop in at any moment for a talk, coming through the window when the family were at meals or by the way which was most convenient.

There was no formality and no privacy at Glenferry, but in Kensington Mrs. Tarn gradually reverted to type, and her family, almost before they were aware of it, were educated to a different code of manners.

After a year or so in London, Pamela and her father no longer invited people to drop in when they felt inclined, and the few acquaintances and friends who had found in the Tarn household something unusual began to remember to telephone before they called or to wait for an invitation.

The girls changed their dresses for the evening meal; Mrs. Tarn expected her husband to come when the gong rang instead of rushing into the room halfway through luncheon or supper, untidy and unwashed but glowing with some new discovery.

Gradually, so slowly that no-one noticed it, a live spirit was being suffocated.

Convention laid a stranglehold on Pamela's father, and she felt now that it was that which had aged him and hastened his death, his spirit glad to escape because it could no longer survive in such an atmosphere.

Ion had also escaped, and Pamela knew that she too, now at the eleventh hour, before the last ultimate surrender of herself, had been awakened and warned of her own danger.

She had shrunk from Cowton, but she realised, when she thought about it, that Cowton was only a luxurious and little less alive edition of what her own home had become.

The importance of trivialities, the monotonous timetable by which the days were measured, and suffocation of anything original or individual, the subjection of personality to the common standards, it was all there as it was in hundreds of thousands of homes all over the country.

Every day children were being born into it, the wings of their spirits being clipped from the very moment of birth until like animals bred in captivity they had no memory of anything outside the confining bars of their cages.

But Pamela had once known with Ion the reality of the enchanted land which is the hereditary right of all who seek it, and now "memories' resurrection" had come to her. . . .

It was growing dark and Pamela was beginning to feel the strain of driving when at last she reached the outskirts of Southampton.

Her eyes were burning and sore and she was glad of the twilight creeping up the sky. She drove slowly through the town, asking her way to the docks.

Finally she found a garage for the car, leaving it there in Arthur's name and asking the owner of the garage to write him a line informing him of the car's safe arrival.

Then, carrying her suitcase, she turned towards the quay. She bought her ticket and made her way on board the ship.

It was early and there were few people about, as the boat-train was not yet due. She put her suitcase down below and went on deck, finding a comfortable seat to windward.

Only in the cessation of movement which she had experienced all day, in the quiet and the reflection of lights on the water below, did she suddenly realise that she was starting a great adventure.

She was travelling alone into an unknown future.

*   *   *

"I tell you straight that if there's a war you won't get no men to fight in it. They're not going to be such damned fools a second time!"

The words, spoken in an aggressive voice—husky, perhaps from excessive smoking or drinking—aroused Pamela to consciousness of her surroundings.

The ship was moving smoothly but slowly down Southampton Water, and though she was still sitting in her sheltered seat her mind was with the Abbot John when he had set forth in the wooden sailing-ship which had carried him, centuries ago, across the Channel.

She felt that she was echoing what must have been his feelings as the frail craft left the shores of the land to which he belonged and set off into the unknown.

It was not of the past that he thought or of those to whom he bade farewell, nor of a future fraught with danger and adventure, but of the present and himself.

He stood, as she did today, in an interval as it were between two acts of a play—an interlude when the curtain has fallen, but with no finality, and when there is a sense of preparation and of a gathering strength for what is to come.

Her own emotions, Pamela thought at this moment, were something like those of good Catholics when, after confession, they receive absolution of past sins.

They come back to the world with what is called a "clean page" in front of them, but what is in reality the power of starting off again on the familiar path unburdened, reassured, and light of heart.

For none of us is there the opportunity to start life afresh; what we have been has made us what we are, and if we journey to the far corners of the world on a new mission, another career, or in search of the yet unknown, we take with us our familiar selves.

A personality is accumulated painstakingly through the years, maybe the centuries.

But we can, and do, find in life oases of rest and refreshment, whence we can take up our pilgrimage with added courage and revived hope.

Like the Abbot John, Pamela felt unburdened, all her strength garnered to face whatever tomorrow might bring.

Her inward concentration was interrupted, and she realised that unnoticed passengers had been passing to and fro and that now three of them had seated themselves near her.

She peered through the shadows and distinguished the first speaker as a small, weedy little man with a lined, disgruntled face, wearing a mackintosh and a cheap cloth cap.

"You talk and talk, but what's it mean?" answered the fat woman who was doubtless his wife.

She was wearing a harassed expression, in spite of her comfortable proportions, and clutching a large patent-leather handbag.

"Wait until the band begins to play," she said, "and then everyone'll get war madness, same as they've done before. You can talk against war, Alfred, till you are blue in the face; but when the time comes I shouldn't be surprised if you were one of the first to go."

"Catch me being such a ruddy fool," her husband answered. "What's more, we shall be beaten within the first week of the next war, and that isn't far distant, neither. We've got no men, we've got no guns, and we've got no aeroplanes."

"We have got something more important than any of those things, though," said the third figure.

Pamela was surprised at his voice, for it was quiet and better-educated than those of the other two speakers.

He rose to his feet and walked to the rail, and she saw that he was a tall man and was smoking a pipe. Something in his bearing, or maybe it was merely her imagination, made her connect him with the Church.

"And what's that, I'd like to know?" Alfred asked him.

"The spirit of righteousness," came the reply.

There was a silence for a moment, as if both Alfred and his wife were surprised; then Alfred's rasping voice jeered back:

"Religious stuff! What d'you mean?"

"Not particularly religious," came the quiet answer—"not what you'd call religion, anyway, but the fact that England and her men don't fight unless they believe the cause they support is one of truth and justice. And that is why, if we go to war, which you seem so certain we shall, we shall win."

"What, with no aeroplanes, no guns, no ammunition and no ships?" shouted Alfred. "We haven't got a ruddy chance."

"As I said before," the tall man replied, "there is something more important than all those things. But I grant you they are necessary in this miserable, mechanical-minded twentieth century.

"But I would rather have a handful of men who were fighting with their hearts and souls than a million who were driven to it because a dictator trained them like animals and like animals drove them before him into the field of battle."

"Them high-falutin' ideas are all very fine," Alfred answered, "but I stick to what I says. If there's a war, you won't get no men to fight in it."

"Do you mean to say," the tall man replied, "that if I hit your wife in the face to take her bag away from her, or if I fetch a child here and torture him in front of your eyes, you will stand by and let me?"

Alfred shuffled his feet.

"That ain't a fair argument," he said. "That's personal, that is."

"When the time comes, every war is a personal one," the tall man said. "And that is why I say that the Army whose soldiers have the spirit of righteousness within them, who know that they are fighting evil, righting a wrong, or delivering the oppressed, is the only Army, however small, however ill-equipped, which will survive, and survive victoriously."

"Fancy words," sneered Alfred. "They don't mean nothing. When a bullet's got you in the guts, you're for it right or wrong, and if we're all killed off, where will your cause of righteousness be then?"

"Just where it was before," the tall man answered.

"A ruddy lot of help that will be," Alfred replied.

"Well, what do you want?" asked the other.

"One moment you are saying you won't fight and the next moment you are complaining because we have not got enough arms to fight with."

"That's true enough," said the woman. "Alfred doesn't know what he wants, that's the trouble. He thinks he is a pacifist, but I don't believe him. It's a lot of talk from those who are frightened, that's what I think."

"You couldn't have put it better," the tall man said with a chuckle.

"Now look here," said Alfred fiercely. "I'm not going to be talked at like that, I can tell you. There'll be a bit of ruddy trouble round here before we've done."

"Oh, stow it, Alfred!" his wife retorted. "Don't let's start the holiday with a quarrel.

"Let's hope the war will keep off until we are back in England, anyway. I'm sure I'm always grateful that the country's an island and you can't wake up one morning and find a lot of foreigners in your back garden. Let's go down below and have a drink."

Grumbling, but obviously used to obeying his better half, Alfred rose and followed her down below.

The tall man stood looking after them for a moment, puffing at his pipe, and then he strode away, his footsteps echoing on the deck.

When they had gone, Pamela sat thinking of them. She somehow felt a sneaking sympathy with Alfred's difficulties.

She too knew how often one's convictions can cross and double-cross one another, becoming more and more contradictory in the process.

Underneath, in all probability he was violently patriotic and, as his wife had said, would be one of the first to fight for his country in the hour of need.

Yet, knowing in his own mind that war was wrong, sensing the uselessness, desolation, and misery of it, he was striving ineffectually to avoid it, as one of the many cogs in a great wheel which must turn because it is commanded or because Fate decrees the movement.

Pamela remembered her father saying:

"How hard it is for individualism to assert itself in any so-called civilised State. For citizenship involves great penalties. It chains men and uses them just as effectively as slaves were chained in years gone by. Only in imagination are men born free today."

The twinkling yellow lights of the Isle of Wight, the golden pathways of reflection stretching from the ship over the dark water, and the glimmer of stars above were to Pamela small things which she noticed subconsciously.

She was not giving her full mind to them, but she knew that they were there and that when looking back she would be able to recall them all.

Once she had wondered whether it was possible to think of two things at once.

Now she knew that her thoughts and brain concentrated on her inward self whilst much else, from without, entered her consciousness and was stored away in the vaults of her memory.

Later Pamela went below and lay down in the saloon.

There were two or three children already sleeping, and women were partially undressing, loosening their clothing and taking off their shoes before arranging themselves on the small bunks.

Pamela would have liked to take a cabin for herself, but it cost two pounds and she could not spare the money; every penny must be saved.

When she finally lay down she realised how tired she was.

No sooner was she comfortable than she fell asleep, and it seemed to her only a few minutes before the stewardess was shaking her shoulder, telling her that it was half-past-six and that they would dock in about half-an-hour. . . .

* * *

The train whistled and creaked its way into St. Malo Station, and although there was plenty of room, passengers pushed and elbowed their way into the carriages.

They were spurred on by that agitated fear which attacks most people when travelling, so that the worst and most disagreeable side of their natures comes to the surface.

The brown wooden seats of the railway carriage were hard and uncomfortable.

Pamela had never before travelled in a French third-class carriage, and after the comfort of well-padded English seats, she wondered, as many people had before her, why a republican country should cater so little to the comfort of its poorer citizens.

Her companions were a large fat Frenchwoman who was wearing the long crêpe veil and hot, sombre garments of widowhood, and a little girl of five who had the sophisticated, anxious look prevalent among French children.

Even when they are babies they have old faces, as though their youth was to be found only in the proportions of their bodies.

The child stared at Pamela with dark, unblinking eyes for most of the journey. Pamela wondered what there was in her appearance to inspire such strange interest.

She smiled once or twice but received no response, and those small dark eyes continuing to watch her critically.

Another passenger was obviously a school-teacher, struggling half-heartedly with a German text-book; she had been burnt by the sun and her skin was the most unbecoming shade of pink.

Two hikers—pleasant-looking youths with knapsacks on their backs, fair-haired, strong-muscled—were typical of the new generation in France which was superseding the traditional small-bodied, dark-haired Frenchmen with their dislike of sports, exercise, and too much fresh air.

After travelling for about two hours Pamela had to change to another train. She had a little time to wait and spent it walking up and down the platform, looking at the strange variety of travellers who crowded out of one train and into another.

There were monks in brown robes and sandals, nuns with starched linen coifs and with huge silver crucifixes dangling from their waists, peasants wrapped in shawls, hikers young and sunburnt, large parties of school-children, and babies in prams.

Finally Pamela's train started, with only a few passengers aboard.

She was alone in her carriage. Putting her feet up on the opposite seat, she made a pillow of her tweed overcoat, and, leaning her head against it, she slept.

She awoke to find herself in Brittany. There were trees, twisted and unpruned but nevertheless bearing golden and red fruit in curiously divided fields with hedgerows, which while common in England was most unusual in France.

There were patches of marshland, twisted, narrow streams winding through willow-bordered banks, and the often-recurring woods of pine trees.

They were dark-shadowed and cool even on the hottest days, their deep green seeming to hold impregnable secrets from the outside world.

It seemed to Pamela then—and later she was to know that Brittany was a secretive country—full of mysteries and of strange reserves, which made it, even in its most beautiful moments, show but little of its innermost self to the observer.

Pamela felt that even those people who loved it most could learn but superficially of it.

It was like an old woman who has forgotten far more than she can remember, but whose full life, whose experience of love and lovers, has developed her into a curious personality attractive even in old age.

Superstitious and religious, the peasants of Brittany have the natural good manners of nature's gentlefolk.

While still in the train Pamela fell in love with their quaint costumes, the high, starched-lace caps of the women worn with full-skirted velvet dresses.

High-spired Churches and the roofs of small towns glittered in the sunlight; and then as the afternoon passed, a faint mist began to cover the landscape.

The mist crept up the wide rivers where ships lay waiting for cargo, and in the air there was a taste of salt and a twang of the sea.

Pamela, leaning out the window, was not surprised to see through the pine trees glimpses of a pale horizon and to know that, for good or for bad, she had reached her destination.

The curtain was rising on another scene of her life.

THE WISDOM OF
DAKSINĀ MŪRTI—STOTRA

The Universe is like the image of a city seen in the depths of the mirror. It arises out of the Self due to illusion. It looks as if the world lies out there.

It is like the objects of the dream that one dreams. On waking up, one realises that all that was seen was those in one's own individual self.

—*Sankara*

Chapter Three

P amela stepped out of the bus at Bugalé, and, having paid four francs—not an exorbitant sum—for the ten miles it had carried her from Quimper where her train journey had ended, she picked up her suitcase and stood looking round her.

She felt, for the first time since she had started, slightly apprehensive.

On one side of the road stood a small grey Church with the usual ornate gravestones, and an ugly, modern, war memorial, its crude, inartistic realism contrasting unfavourably with the weather-beaten beauty of the ancient statues which surmounted the Church door.

Beyond the Church-yard and round it were pine trees growing in sandy soil to the very edge of the dunes which sloped to the sea.

On the other side of the narrow main road was the rest of the village—a few simple fishermen's cottages, one or two of them thatched and all of them whitewashed, with tiny gardens ablaze with hydrangeas and dahlias.

The one shop bore a sign in scarlet lettering that read: AU GALERIE DE BUGALÉ and was reached by climbing steps with an ornate iron balustrade painted a vivid green.

Beyond the shop and the cottages was the local

Inn. Over the open door was the sign: AU BON ACCUEIL.

Outside, on two wooden benches were seated several worthies of the village—old men wearing the high, velvet, buttoned waistcoats of peasant Brittany, and wide-brimmed black hats trimmed with velvet ribbon and held by silver buckles.

At the side of the building itself was a garden containing chairs and tables and, surprisingly, a dusty but sturdy palm tree.

There was no-one eating, for it was already afternoon, but bright-coloured soda-syphons stood on several of the tables and a waitress wearing a beribboned lace cap moved briskly in and out of the Inn, carrying a tray piled with dirty glasses.

Slowly Pamela moved towards the Inn, forming in her mind the sentences with which she would enquire for Ion.

She felt shy and lacking in confidence now that the moment was actually upon her. To herself she seemed a slightly ridiculous figure, out-of-place and rather overdressed in these primitive surroundings.

The old men stared solemnly at her, while at their feet a mangy dog scratched itself, then rolled backwards and forwards with its legs in the air.

A sudden fear that they might speak only Breton, and therefore not understand her French, made her hesitate and walk a little way past them.

As she did so, a girl carrying a plate of food in one hand and a large mug of cider in the other came out of a side door of the Inn, passed through the garden, and started to cross the roadway.

Without further hesitation Pamela walked up to her.

"Can you tell me," she asked in French, "if Mr. Ion Tarn is staying anywhere in the village?"

"Yes, he is," the girl answered calmly.

But Pamela was conscious that the girl was instantly on the defensive.

"Can you tell me where I can find him?" Pamela asked.

"Why do you want him?" the girl enquired.

She stared at Pamela and seemed surprised.

"Surely," she ejaculated, "surely you must be . . ."

"His sister," Pamela finished for her.

"You are so alike," the girl said. "It is extraordinary. I am Lisette. He is across here. I was just taking him some food. Will you come with me?"

Pamela followed her, still carrying her suitcase. She glanced at her companion as they walked towards the pine trees.

She was a small, slender girl, with dark hair which was parted in the centre and curled round the nape of her neck but was brushed back from the ears to show two large, circular, gold ear-rings.

Round her neck she wore an orange and green handkerchief loosely knotted, which with a crimson woollen jumper gave her a picturesque gipsy appearance.

She did not smile at Pamela; and in her silence and her calm acceptance of her arrival there was a dignity which made Pamela feel young and inexperienced, while at the same time she was quite sure that this girl was only her own age if not younger.

Almost as soon as they entered the pine trees Pamela saw, facing the shore, enclosed on three sides and protected by the trees, a rough shack, little more than a shed, which in other surroundings might have been used for cattle.

It had an entrance at the rear and a strongly made roof which looked capable of withstanding any weather.

As they reached the door Lisette paused and put down the mug of cider while she lifted the latch.

As she did so, she gave Pamela a long, searching glance from under dark, curling eye-lashes, and then still without a word she entered, leaving the door open for Pamela to follow.

Inside, there were rough, uneven floorboards to walk on. A large divan which stretched across the threshold almost barred their entrance, and beyond it Pamela saw the shoulders and head of a man.

His back was towards them and he was silhouetted against wide-open windows facing the sea.

Their footsteps vibrated on the wooden floor as Lisette advanced and Pamela, moving round the divan, put down her suitcase.

Pamela was conscious that her heart was thumping.

Without looking up, Ion said:

"For God's sake, keep away! Can't you see I'm working?"

Lisette did not answer. She laid beside him the plate on which, Pamela saw, was a lobster salad, set the mug of cider on the table, then stood looking at Pamela as though in silent introduction.

Ion glanced up irritably, turned, and saw who stood behind him. For a moment brother and sister looked steadily at each other.

A swift smile then came to Ion's lips.

"Pamela!" he said. "By all that's wonderful! And you are just the person I want. I can't get this. Listen."

He rose to his feet, holding the paper on which he had been writing, and moved towards the window, leaning against the lintel and running his free hand through his dark, untidy hair.

Without a word or another look Lisette moved

from beside the table and walked from the hut, closing the door behind her.

Pamela sat down on a chair as Ion started to read:

"There is a spirit of war abroad.
I smell it in the wind which blows over the cornfield,
I hear it in the rumbling of the thunder in the hills,
I feel it in the quiver and the trembling of the earth
Beneath the heavy tread of marching feet.
There is a spirit of war abroad!"

Ion let the paper drop.

"This is where I am stuck," he said despondently. "I have another line here:

"In women there is a fever of expectancy.

"But I can't put into words what men feel about war. Perhaps it is because I am too close to it, feeling it myself.

"I can see and understand the women; that waiting, fearfully, intently, for something which will shatter and destroy their homes and yet which to them, while horrible and terrifying, is still a kind of queer excitement.

"But men don't anticipate things in the same way. I can see their faces, taut and almost expressionless because the emotion they feel must not be shown, and yet that doesn't express what I want to say. Tell me, Pamela, how do men await the news of war?"

Ion's eyes were flashing as he talked, and he moved his hands in gestures that were as forcible as words.

Pamela felt utterly at her ease, not so much taking up the threads of their friendship where it had left off but merely continuing an association which

had never been broken, however separated they may
have been physically.

Between Ion and herself there had always been
some bond or inner harmony, far stronger than, and
utterly independent of, their nearness.

As children she had never thought it strange that
in a day or afternoon spent apart she should be
aware of Ion's mood long before evening united them
and he was there to tell her of his feelings.

Ion had never needed to tell his sister about
himself.

She knew, and in some feminine, adaptable
manner could alter herself to what he required of
her, giving him not equality, for he would not have
wished for that, but rather a reverse of his own emotions, so that his strength could be accentuated by
her frailty, or his courage increased by her fear.

It had been a perfect companionship, in that
Pamela was the weaker counterpart of Ion.

Then as they grew older she was aware that
there was something more which she could give him,
a strength of her own, a clarity of direction, so that
when in contact with her he could find expression.

She was the transmitter of the music of his
thoughts.

Although in those days he had not been creative
or else had nothing to show for his imagination, within him there was always some process of construc-
tion taking place.

Often Pamela alone could smooth the chaos for
him, simplify the entangling, tortuous way of his
visions.

This she did unconsciously and gently, for children always accept miracles with serenity.

Now, his problem having been placed before
her, she concentrated on it, knowing the harmony

that was between them and aware that once again she was taking her appointed place in his life.

'His brain,' she thought, 'is like a delicate instrument beneath my fingers.'

She was confident that she could strike the right note.

"Coming over on the boat," she said slowly, pulling off her small, silk-stitched hat and dropping it on the floor beside her, "there were two men talking beside me, and they spoke of war. One argued against it, and yet asked for greater armaments and more guns, not sure of what he wanted, and, I think, secretly afraid. The other—"

"Wait a moment," Ion said, striding up and down the room. "Men argue without conviction, without faith, without knowledge. . . . Never mind. The idea is clearing . . . I see him. Go on."

"And the other," Pamela continued, "spoke of a spirit of righteousness, saying that England must win because of it—implying, I think, that even being killed does not matter so long as the cause is just."

"I see that too," Ion said, his eyes half-closed in an effort of concentration. "Fools justifying a fool's action, founding truth on false foundations. Yes, I've got it now; the words will come later."

He crumpled the paper on which he had been writing and threw it into a corner of the room.

Then, as if he cast all thoughts and difficulties behind him, he walked across to Pamela and, putting his hands on her shoulders, looked down into her face.

"It is good to see you again," he said. "Have you altered? Yes, you are lovelier, but there is something . . ."

His eyes searched her face.

"You don't look so peaceful, so . . . no, that isn't

right . . . you don't look so sure. That's what I always clung to about you, a quality which I never had. Life never seemed to startle you, while I was in a continual state of bewilderment at every turn."

Pamela smiled.

"And you," she said. "Let me look at you."

He had gone away from her a boy who was old for his age—or, rather, ageless, for all people who are intuitively and spiritually alive are too wise for their bodies; now she found him a man.

The years which had passed had left deep lines on his face and had sharpened and accentuated the look of eagerness which was almost synonymous with a hunger, not for food but for knoweldge.

Yet at the same time he had retained that strange faculty of seeming like a lamp, lit now and then by a flame, or becoming, when his interest was unawakened, just the structure of something which had once been alive.

Even in his most depleted moments one was always conscious that presently the light would return and once again he would be glowingly alive.

Pamela wondered what he had suffered and what he had experienced when he had sought his freedom, depriving himself of every material support and help.

But it was characteristic of their relationship that she did not question him but started, unasked, to explain her coming.

"I read your book," she said, "the night before last. It came to me just in time. I had almost forgotten."

"And so you ran away too," he said. "It comes to all of us, I suppose."

And then, as though there were nothing more to say about the situation, he picked up the pile of closely written paper on one side of his desk and held it towards her.

"This is my new book," he said, "but I have approached much of it from the wrong angle. You must tell me where I ought to begin."

"Who is Lisette?" Pamela asked abruptly, taking the manuscript from him but not looking at it.

"Why do you ask that so suddenly?" Ion asked.

"I was only wondering," Pamela answered; "hoping that she wouldn't mind my coming here, if she is in a position to mind."

Ion laughed.

"I believe you are jealous," he said, "just as you were years ago at Glenferry of little Sheila Whatever-her-name-was—the girl with red hair."

"MacFarlane."

"I remember you pulling her plaits and scratching her face when she tried to kiss me."

"She was a horrible child," Pamela retorted.

Then they both laughed.

It was quite true, she had been jealous of him, resenting his interest in red hair and freckles, and an openly expressed admiration, a flattery which he had been unable to resist.

Ion's supremacy in Pamela's heart had no rival. The only other person she loved was her father, and the affection she had given him was in no way comparable to that which she gave her brother.

In London, Pamela was continually surprised by the attitude of her contemporaries towards their parents.

While Pamela adored her father, she never for one moment expected him to stoop towards a mental equality with her or to consider that the difference between their ages could be bridged by common interests.

Her adoration held an admiration and a respect which would have been quite impossible for her to give to a contemporary, and which enlarged rather than restricted her love.

Love that has in it a touch of worship springs from the very highest and noblest impulse in man.

Pamela's love for her father was but a parallel, in a simpler and less intense form, with the simplicity of primitive religion in which mankind makes God in his own image, glorifying and deifying the highest standard of his own imagination.

Her father and her brother therefore received from Pamela a love which, while entirely different, seemed to stretch to the uttermost bounds her capability of giving.

While she approached her father on her knees, she walked side by side with Ion, finding with him the true meaning of companionship and its real interpretation: "They who know and help, they who are and are of one another."

Thinking of Glenferry made Pamela ask Ion a question which had often been uppermost in her mind.

"When will you go back home?" she said; it was significant that she said "when," and "home" needed no explanation.

"Not yet," Ion answered. "I have a feeling that the time will come and that I shall know it, rather like waiting for death, not death as physical decay but death as a release, as a fulfilment.

"That is what I feel about Glenferry—that I cannot go back until I have travelled and journeyed to the end and await only the finality of completion."

Pamela was silent for a moment, then she said:

"When Father was dying I was in his room one morning and there was sunshine outside, although it was November, and suddenly he said:

"'There is a mist now, but it will be clear later.'

"Mother was in the room; she thought his eyes were failing, and she pulled back the curtains a little way, signalling to me not to answer him.

"But I knew that he was not lying in that ugly, low-ceilinged little room in Kensington; he was at Glenferry and he was seeing, as we have so often seen, the mist lying on the hill-tops in the morning before the sun comes out to drive it away.

"He died a few hours later; he was smiling, and I knew that for him the sunlight had come out at Glenferry and was shining silver on the river and the sea was blue."

"I shall go back," Ion said quietly.

*   *   *

Lisette walked from the shack back to the garden of the Inn.

In a far corner, on a chair set in the shade, she had left her knitting, a bundle of bright emerald-green wool from which she was making a jumper.

When she had nearly reached it she glanced up to find, sitting at a nearby table, half-concealed behind the thick foliage of a pear tree, an elderly man with a short grey beard.

He had a book open in front of him but he was not reading. Instead, he was staring ahead in meditation, and at the same time he was filling his short and ancient pipe from the pouch beside him.

Lisette picked up her work, drew her chair nearer to his, and after a few stitches she spoke, her voice casual and without inflection.

"Ion's sister has arrived," she said.

She spoke in English and the elderly man answered her in the same language, but his accent was quite different from hers—guttual, his voice low and full, yet melodious.

"So!" he said. "And what is she like?"

"Beautiful," Lisette answered. "And so like Ion that I recognised her at once. She has his look, too— that haunted expression as if they were trying to remember something they had once known."

"Why has she come?" the man asked.

Lisette shrugged her shoulders.

"I tell you she is like Ion," she answered; "in which case she will have no explanation. He never has."

"Not one we can understand, perhaps," the man answered.

Lisette glanced up at him—a questioning look which at the same time held an acknowledgement that he probably was right.

Had she disagreed with him, Lisette would not have said so, for part of her charm—for men, at any rate—was the fact that she never argued and seldom asserted her opinion.

She was a strange person indeed, and her unusualness made her attractive to most of the men with whom she came in contact.

Ion never commented or seemed surprised by her, but accepted her, as she loved him, without criticism.

Lisette, whose real name was Yvonne Grécamp, had been the mistress of several men before she had met Ion.

Her mother was caretaker of a large block of studios in the Latin Quarter of Paris, and since childhood she had been brought up to understand, to cater to, and to like men.

At the age of seven she had started to sit for

artists, her mother being only too glad to have the extra money.

As she grew older her unusual looks made her the fashion as a model, and with success her price for sitting grew correspondingly high.

However, much to her mother's annoyance, Lisette would allow no monetary advantage to override her inclinations, and if she did not care for an artist, no bribe was large enough to make her sit for him.

She was more than just a model to the men whom she met; to a certain extent she inspired them in their work, urging them towards success and often helping them in her own way.

She had the sound, balanced mind of a Parisian, knowing the true value of what is for sale and the way to show goods to their best advantage.

Many a struggling young artist owed the sale of his pictures entirely to her, and she would work for the success of a man while she spurned his physical advances and laughed at his protestations of affection.

Artists were not the only people who lodged in the flats and studios under her mother's charge.

There were students of all sorts, and she would help them with their studies so that for her own education she acquired an extraordinary assortment of miscellaneous facts, storing them in her mind rather as a magpie might collect a strange variety of articles.

To Ion, Lisette's knowledge was a never-ending source of interest, and he would listen to her until some extraordinary statement of hers would delight him as a small boy who has just discovered treasure-trove.

Lisette, at seventeen, had more young men desiring her than is good for the character of any young girl, however hard her upbringing.

She lost her heart and her virtue to a middle-aged Swedish artist, whose studio she shared for nearly two years until his habit of drinking himself insensible finally destroyed her affection for him.

However, when he was sober he was a highly cultured, well-educated man, and in spite of his shortcomings he taught Lisette much; most important of all, he instilled in her a taste in manners and in behaviour.

In the extraordinary contradiction of human nature, it was not strange that this man, who would lie semi-sensible after a debauch lasting twenty-four hours, could become almost frenzied at any *gaucherie* or vulgarity.

From him Lisette learnt her repose, her quiet voice, and a refinement which, though born naturally within her, had been entirely undeveloped.

When she was young she had been called Lisette after a comic and slightly indecent song which gained much popularity in Paris at the time, and until she met Sven she had tried to live up to the roguish, almost raffish ideal of her name.

A girl in her first love is as pliable in a man's hands as a child in the first seven years of its life.

Sven was a gentleman, and he tamed Lisette kindly, so that when he finally passed from her life he left her with a high standard of herself, as well as a critical attitude towards other men.

This was certainly to the good, for Lisette's attractions had developed so that she had no difficulty in finding a protector to take Sven's place.

They were there in scores, willingly offering her not only their hearts and careers but their names as well, if she so desired.

But Lisette had no intention of deciding her future in a hurry.

She went back to live with her mother for a little while, and then, finding her garrulity too much for peace, she chose from her many admirers a young Irish painter who optimistically hoped to one day make enough money to return to his own Isle.

Pat O'Brien did not drink, but he had other detractions which made life with him almost unbearable.

He was so jealous that he could not bear to have Lisette out of his sight even for a moment, and he would pick a quarrel with the *gendarme* on point duty should she smile at him while crossing the road.

It was an eventful year that she spent with him, and her memory of it was of fierce, burning, bitter words, of blows struck in the heat of anger, of tears and repentance, and of a happiness which was all the more intense because of its brevity.

Whenever she thought of Pat she seemed to taste kisses with salty tears, to think of his love as a torrential sea which, while it enfolded her, battered and bruised her cruelly upon rocks.

She could never have left Pat, for he would have followed her to the end of the world and forced her back into his arms, but he was taken from her by the law and sent to prison for fifteen years following a charge of manslaughter.

For once the fight was not over her personally; she had not been with him at the time.

But when he had been taken away from her— haggard, white-faced, but still indomitably truculent —she had realised almost with relief that for the first time in months she could call her life her own.

Having learnt from Pat to be afraid of life, Lisette did not commit herself for some months to the embraces of any passion which might again hold her prisoner.

Then, in violent reaction against her own prudity, she fell very much in love with an Englishman who was many years her senior who in some ways reminded her of Sven.

Jimmy Drayton was in Paris for the simple reason that he had been in such trouble in England that he did not dare to show his face there again for some years.

While he had great attractions, he was unstable and had an inherent dishonesty which made him prefer to take what he wanted by any but honest methods.

He had the charm of an adventurer, the proverbial stumbling-block of most women. It is because such men have courage and a disregard of conventions that they appeal to the vagabond spirit in women as respectability and security never can.

Since the beginning of the world men have complained that women love cads and bounders.

It is because in an adventurer there is a romance and a devil-may-care joy which calls to all that is wild and unstable in the feminine.

Girls ran after Jimmy as the children ran after the Pied Piper of Hamelin—they could not resist him—and when he wanted Lisette there was not the slightest hope that she could withstand him.

For some time they were extraordinarily happy. He loved her with an intensity which amounted almost to ecstasy, which was quite unlike anything she had known before.

He was sensuous in a way which made her love her own beauty because it gave him pleasure.

His very extravagances of passion made her proud rather than ashamed and gave her a new standard physically as Sven had given her a new standard mentally.

But actually Jimmy had one use, and one use only, for women.

He desired nothing from them; but they aroused him to sexual rapture and supplied an audience to whom he could show off his charm and brilliance as a peacock spreads its tail.

He was, as he had always been in past love-affairs, uninterested in Lisette except as an acquisition to himself, and thus, after a while, though in his own fashion he still wanted her, he was unfaithful to her when the opportunity came.

Keeping women from Jimmy would have been as impossible as trying to grow flowers without sunlight.

They were necessary to him, and Lisette began to suffer the tortures of pride and self-accusation which all women go through when the man they love betrays them.

The fact that Lisette was his wife made little or no difference to him.

He had married her on an impulse which came fundamentally from his desire to show off, to behave as it were in a grand style.

His proposal of marriage had been a magnificent gesture, the condescension of a great man taking a defenceless woman into his keeping. Jimmy was always acting, even to himself.

He saw himself in the rôle of a dashing Englishman abroad, marrying the beautiful French gamine who would lisp broken English at him in her astonishment at his generosity.

That Lisette did not lisp, and that with her composure she could hardly be called an astonished gamine, did not deter him from this picture, which for a long time he retained pleasantly in his mind.

Jimmy played at poverty in a top-floor flat which had a view over the roofs of Paris, just as in England he had played with the idea of being a millionaire with money he did not possess.

Finally poverty began to bore him.

When his enjoyment from exhibiting himself courageously and indomitably in an attic began to pall, when supplies of food and drink became equivalent to his poverty, and his appearance began to lose its smartness, he revolted.

A nostalgia for the Ritz, for bars where he could find old acquaintances, giving him the chance to borrow and very likely to rob them in one way or another, made him spend less and less time in Lisette's company.

The day came when she returned from shopping to find the flat divested of all Jimmy's belongings and a note on the table telling her that she was not likely to see him again.

Dry-eyed and confiding in no-one, she returned to her mother. The agony she felt was softened by her knowledge of the many times that her husband had been unfaithful.

As the months passed she seemed to her acquaintances little altered and certainly not unhappy, although her reserve was impenetrable against all their questions, however tactfully phrased.

Then she met Ion.

Quite suddenly he had come into her life and equally suddenly she had realised that this was the man for whom she had been waiting, for whom she had in some mysterious way been preparing herself through all the vicissitudes she had known and experienced.

It was as if the other men she had loved had been but an education, fitting her for Ion.

They had met casually, for Fate seldom warns us that we are coming to the cross-roads when past and present separate into an unexpected future.

The second time they had met Ion said to her:

"I am going to Switzerland tonight. Are you coming with me?"

When she had answered "Yes," their eyes met with an understanding which needed no words to augment it.

Ion desired her fiercely, commanding her complete surrender to him.

He found in those dark nights in the little wooden chalet high up in the mountains that she could respond to him with a fire as brilliant and as burning as his own.

Delighted, he had let the days and nights drift by while Lisette taught him much of love.

Then, just as quickly, the desire for creation was upon him and he turned from her, forgetful of all save his work, and another but no less fierce fire consumed him until he dropped asleep where he sat, his head falling forward on scrawled paper, his hands still holding his pencil.

Strangely enough, Lisette understood.

She knew that she had been the stimulus, the incentive to this energy, and she was content to wait until, barren, he would return to her so that once again she could revive in him the flame which was never spent but only dimmed.

There was indeed a part of Ion which she could not understand and to which she could not grow near. It was as if she were a priestess guarding and tending a Temple into which she could not enter.

There was a veil she was not privileged to lift, and she was sufficiently wise not to try to possess this finality of him, but to accept his escape.

It was here that her experience in the past stood her in good stead. She had learnt patience, and she had learnt to give herself completely; her strength lay in her selflessness.

She became a part of Ion's life, a necessary part, and he turned to her in need as a man who is cold goes immediately towards the fire.

She had no idea when such moments might arrive.

Sometimes when he seemed closest to her, their very love was an inspiration which drove him away.

Once, at a time when an insatiable passion enfolded them both so that the days and nights passed like some golden dream, she had stood waiting for him, the moon shining on her through the uncurtained windows while she looked out on a land turned silver by its light.

She had trembled a little, waiting for the first sound of Ion's footfall, for the touch of his hand on the handle of the door.

When at last he had entered she turned swiftly towards him, her face alight with love, her hands going out towards him in welcome.

The moonlight shining through the transparency of her nightgown, throwing into relief the slender, lissom lines of her figure, had held him for a moment spellbound with her beauty.

She was like some sprite, some legendary figure such as men dream of, and which some try ineffectually to capture with pen and paint.

Ion was suddenly still, seeming hardly to breathe, his eyes staring at her with that same awe and amazement which lights the expression of those who see a vision.

When finally with a strange sound in his throat, as one who finds no words, he clasped her in his arms, Lisette knew that in that moment he had escaped her.

His love had passed from and beyond her, soaring where she could not follow, not even in imagination, and when in the hours that followed she held him to her, it was only a body that was hers.

Long before the dawn broke she lay alone, silent and uncomplaining, while Ion wrote feverishly, driven by that power within him which must when conceived instantly seek creation.

THE WISDOM OF THE DATTĀTREYA

The whole Universe is nothing but the five elements. It is similar to the water superimposed on the rays of the Sun. To whom indeed shall I pay my salutation?

I am the only being that is defectless. The world is of earth, fire, water, air and ether. It is only an appearance like water in a mirage. It is not reality.

What forms the self of the individual being is therefore reality. Reality is the Lord, the Self or Dattātreya. It is the defectless identity. There is, therefore, nothing other than itself as the object of its worship.

—*The philosophy of the Avadhuta—Gita*

Chapter Four

Lisette hardly glanced up from her knitting as Ion and Pamela emerged from the shadow of the pine trees and crossed the road towards Au Bon Accueil.

It was her companion who said: "See! They come!"—a fact of which she had been aware from the first moment that the shack door had opened for brother and sister to step forth.

They were walking arm in arm, and linked together they came to the table where the watchers sat.

Ion, putting his free hand on the elderly man's shoulder, said:

"Hans, this is my sister."

Hans Schaeffer rose to his feet and shook hands with Pamela, his eyes searching her face as he did so until with satisfaction he turned to Lisette and remarked:

"You were right, my dear. They are very alike."

Pamela laughed as she sat down.

"It is strange that you should say that," she said. "I have never before thought of there being any strong resemblance between Ion and myself, and yet it seems that there must be a very definite one.

"Am I the one who is supposed to be flattered or are you, Ion?" she said, addressing her brother with a smile.

He answered her vaguely; and then, with the easy grace and the unselfconsciousness of a man who seldom worries about outside opinion, he walked over to Lisette and, putting his hand under her chin, lifted her face towards him.

He did not kiss her, only looked for a moment into her eyes and then rested his cheek against hers in a caress so natural and gentle that there was a quick beauty about it which made the spectators feel a sudden stinging of tears.

There was silence for a moment, then Hans said: "Tell me, my son, how goes the work?"

"Not so well," Ion said, half-despondent.

He sat down at the table and ran his fingers through his hair in a gesture of despair.

"I get periods when although I can see and visualise quite clearly what I want, I can find no words in any known language to express it."

"Ah!" said Hans. "That is where music always has the advantage. It is the language of the gods and need not concern itself with words, which are but poor vehicles to express emotion."

"It is not so much emotion," Ion replied, "that I find difficult to express, but personality. I like my portraits to be strong and clear, yet simple and concise."

"That is where books are all wrong, or rather an impossible medium," Hans said. "You meet a person, you like him or dislike him, it doesn't matter; and all that he has done, everything he has acquired, experienced, or felt, makes him what he is.

"Forty years, fifty years, of living and becoming, and then as an author you try to convey that whole character in two or three short sentences. It is impossible.

"Were I to write fiction I should find that each

puppet of my imagination required a volume to himself so that I could portray him honestly and completely to the reader."

"No, no, Hans, you are wrong!" Ion said hotly. "That is a Teutonic characteristic, your desire for detail, which like many of your countrymen you think important. A good writer separates the essentials of a personality from all that is superficial and unnecessary.

"The fact that a man gets up at eight o'clock in the morning, cleans his teeth with a certain brand of tooth-paste, has eggs and bacon for breakfast and prefers coffee to tea, does not affect one way or another the real man, the personality that the writer is trying to portray.

"Nor does the fact that he is a bastard, or that he was educated as a tight-rope–walker, or that at the age of sixteen he seduced an Inn-keeper's daughter.

"Those things are all unessential unless they play their part in a story. It is what has affected the man himself, the moments when he has risen to heaven or gone down to hell, that alter and mould the vibrations which affect you when you meet him and which makes you consider him or dismiss him as a nonentity.

"There may be nothing tremendous or revolutionary about such moments. For instance, a fly crawling over a plate of ham may start a chain of thoughts or circumstances within a man which becomes completely volcanic and eruptive to all that was there before.

"It is that which the creative artist must capture. Your detailed description of a man in his green Homburg hat and well-cut plus-fours, of his daily habits, is like a police dossier with an attached photograph.

"You read it, you look at the photograph, but does it make you feel anything about the man? No. You visualise him photographically, that is all.

"But my business is to create a living and breathing character, as alive and animate in words as though you met the living man face to face, shook him by the hand, and had a conversation with him. Then you judge him intuitively, your reactions to him being physical."

"Don't you see what Ion means?" Pamela interrupted eagerly.

She had been listening intently to every word her brother said.

"When I read *The Forgotten City* I felt that I knew the Abbot John. I felt that I was reading about someone who had been a friend of mine and for whom I had actual affection. Never for one moment was he an interesting character or just a figment of an author's imagination. He seemed as real as Ion himself."

Hans laughed.

"I am defeated," he said. "I cannot write what I do not feel."

"But surely, when you come down to it," said Pamela ruminatively, frowning a little as she contrated, which made her resemble Ion even more than usual, "you can never create a personality in literature except yourself, because everyone's imagination is different, some small, some large.

"The portrait of your hero or heroine depends on the reader's grasp of him or her. However vital the description, their reactions to it will make it quite unlike your original conception and intention."

"That is true enough," Ion replied. "But one must never ask from man more than he personally is capable of. His understanding of you and your book is bounded of course by his capabilities.

"He can assimilate no more and no less than he is able to; and however great or vital your message, the man to whom you offer it will only retain the infinitesimal part which interests him, if even that much.

"Isn't that what Christ said: 'He that has ears to hear, let him hear'? But to everyone the highest in them will seem divine; and who can judge how high or low divinity may be?"

"There are no words," Hans murmured, "to express divinity or real beauty."

"Not to express it, but to create it, yes. When you write your articles, Hans, when you speak, you use words which inflame and excite the people who hear them.

"The Egyptians thought such eloquence was magic. The words which had such an emotional effect on people were kept secret. They were sacred.

"Only the Priests knew them, and they confined them to ceremonies to which only initiates were admitted. I try to use the same magic, stimulating not the hearts but the souls of men."

"It is not the same for me," Hans said. "My words are meant to be a light, the light of truth, showing the dirt and darkness to those who hitherto have not been able to see.

"But I will not argue," he continued, rising rather heavily to his feet. "I will fetch my loved one and will play to you a little, if you have finished your work for the day."

He walked slowly into the Inn, and when he had gone Lisette spoke for the first time.

"You must not argue with him, Ion," she said. "I

have told you before that he is not well and it worries him. He lies awake thinking over such conversations long after they are past."

"The trouble with Hans," Ion replied, "is that in spite of his life he has no imagination."

Then, as Lisette looked at him in surprise, he added:

"Do you think I am wrong? I am not. He is infinitely compassionate, but it is not the same thing. His feelings and emotions are torn and tortured by the sympathy he feels for those who are oppressed or downtrodden. He feels only what he sees, and never what he does not behold with his own eyes."

"Who is he?" Pamela asked. "Tell me about him."

"You don't know?" Ion said, turning round in amazement to face her. "But no, I had forgotten. The purlieus of respectable Kensington would not have heard of Hans, the man with the voice of fire."

"Oh, but wait!" Pamela exclaimed. "Now that you say that, it comes back to me. Isn't he an agitator, an anarchist, or something like that?"

"Something like that," Ion repeatedly ironically.

But before he could say more Hans came back, carrying a violin tenderly in his hands. He was a big man, but he held the instrument as gently as if it were a child.

He sat down at the table and, tucking his handkerchief under his chin, started to play. Lisette did not stop knitting.

Ion leant forward in his wooden chair, his elbows on the table, his chin resting in his hands. As he listened, his expression relaxed and he looked younger and at peace.

The music was light German airs of long ago, scenes of boyhood, of spring on the Rhine; the tunes which every German loves, those which make every exiled son of the Fatherland feel homesick when he hears them.

Pamela did not know then that Hans had once sworn never to make his "well-beloved," as he called his violin, sob and throb to unhappy music.

This was his relaxation, his escape from the troubles and tribulations which he found were increasingly part of his normal existence. Every man must have relief, some tenderness to soothe him, whatever his circumstances.

"I am lucky," he said once, "that my better half requires so little sustenance and is so frugal a voyager. A new string now and then is all she demands of me, and I need never be jealous that she gives happiness not only to me but to others."

That was true enough, for, as he played, heads appeared at the windows of the Inn and a little crowd of passers-by leant against the low stone wall which bordered the garden, listening, and when he stopped they asked for more.

'How strange this is!' Pamela thought to herself.

Forty-eight hours ago she had been at Cowton Hall, listening to Sir Henry, feeling that nothing unusual could ever occur in that conventional atmosphere, and now she was here, a part of a new and vital community.

Ion's calm acceptance of her presence, his lack of interest in what had brought her there, but his joy in her coming, made her feel more at home than any exaggerated or fulsome welcome would have done.

Even in Lisette's silence she knew there was no antagonism; it was merely that Lisette had no interest in anything or anyone but herself and Ion.

Hans Schaeffer she did not yet understand. She watched him as he played, feeling that here was

someone extraordinarily interesting, quite unlike anyone she had met before.

His grey hair was clipped to the shape of his
large head, and his deep-set eyes were tender now as
he played; he was a Jew, though she doubted if na-
tionality affected him as it did other men.

A faint scent of flowers mingled with the tang of
the sea and the resin of the many pine trees. Bugalé
was a place of peace, as the sun sank lower behind
the trees and the gentle twilight crept over the sea.

Pamela was conscious that she had found no
place of rest but rather one where she would be stimulated and invigorated, a place of conception, perhaps—but for what she had still to discover.

Inside, the Inn was spotlessly clean. The floors of
wood had been scrubbed until the boards were white,
and the windows of the tiny, low-ceilinged bed-rooms
looked out under the thatch towards the sea.

Pamela had a room next to that of Ion and Lisette, for only when he was working did he sleep on
the divan in the little shack on the edge of the shore.

"Did he build the hut there?" Pamela asked, as
Lisette showed her her bed-room.

"Oh, no," Lisette replied. "We couldn't have af-
forded that. Some painter who was here before built
it, and the Inn-keeper is delighted to let it. It is very
cheap—that is why Ion stays on. We have never before been in the same place for nearly a year."

"And you like it?" Pamela asked.

"I am always happy with Ion," Lisette replied.

"I hope you don't mind me staying a little
while?" Pamela asked hesitatingly.

She felt slightly embarrassed at her own words,
yet she was anxious to make friends with someone
Ion loved.

"You help Ion. That is good," said Lisette, her

accent surely more noticeable, as if she too was embarrassed.

"You see," Pamela tried to explain, "after I had read *The Forgotten City* I felt I must see him. So I ran away the night before last, from the man I had promised to marry, and from his home. I felt that I must. Do you understand?"

"Oh, but I do very well," Lisette said warmly, with a smile which made her almost beautiful. "I too have made up my mind so quickly that there has been no time for anything but to go. And this man you were engaged to, will he be very unhappy?"

"I don't know," Pamela said. "I suppose he loves me, and yet it was not . . ."

She hesitated, wondering how she could compare Arthur's deep but unemotional affection for her with the love she wanted and felt was possible for herself.

"Oh, but you are so like Ion," Lisette said. "He too thinks there is only one type of love; but he is wrong. There are many, many sorts, and when they happen one cannot say that this is right or this is wrong. They are all alike yet all different, and all are very precious."

Lisette spoke quietly, but her voice vibrated, and for the first time Pamela understood Ion's need of her. She had depth and a reserve which would intrigue him as long as underneath there was fire to respond to his own.

A gay, vivacious woman would have bored him and irritated him in a few days. Repose is a virtue to be found in few women. Few men require it of them, but Ion was Gaelic and never garrulous even in his childhood.

That, indeed, was the one difference between Ion and Pamela and their younger brothers and sister. The boys and Jean were forever chattering in the natural way of children.

They were afraid of Ion when he was uncommunicative, perhaps in one of his worst moods, speaking but a few sentences the whole day.

Children, like animals, want to be talked to. It is not so much what is said as the mere sound of a voice which gives them confidence and a weak pleasure.

The loneliness which had oppressed Elizabeth Tarn when she first married seemed to have re-created itself in her two eldest children, so that from the moment of their birth they were content with solitude.

They were independent even as babies, and even in their helplessness she felt isolated from them.

There is some strange faculty in women, not yet understood, which often makes them nurture in their children those qualities which they most dislike.

It is as a man may be attracted physically by those very qualities in a woman or a friend which he despises and disdains within his own mind. So is the body eternally at war with the spirit.

When she was alone in her tiny bed-room Pamela stood looking out to sea.

She could hear the waves breaking gently on the sandy shore and could see a few small coloured-sailed fishing-boats coming slowly into the harbour before nightfall.

The coastline, curving away into the distance, was beautiful, the sand shimmering grey beneath an opalescent sky in which already there was the first faint outline of a new moon.

She wanted to possess it all, to hold it within her, yet, even as she desired it, she knew that not yet were the doors of herself wide open.

They were ajar, but there was much to come,

more chains to be cast aside, before she could find her freedom.

* * *

Hans Schaeffer came slowly up the uncarpeted wooden stairs to bed.

He walked as quietly as age and his large body would allow him, for already the little Inn was in darkness, each bed-room door closed, and the bar with its array of bottles of all shapes and sizes was empty and shuttered for the night.

In his room, which was one in a row and identical to the other front bed-rooms of the house, he did not undress for some time, but stood in the dark, looking through the open window.

Hans was not tired. His mind was ceaselessly concerning itself with an article which he was in the midst of writing.

It lay half-finished on the table beside his bed, and he wondered, as he glanced over the closely penned sentences, where it was likely to be printed, for his market was becoming more and more restricted.

From Germany he was an exile. The Nazis had done their best to be rid of him, on one occasion kidnapping him while he was in Switzerland and driving him towards the frontier.

After a few days in prison he would, he knew, have been sentenced to death.

He escaped, but not before such punishment had been inflicted upon him as to seriously undermine his health and affect his heart, so that the doctor who examined him in Paris had given a very open verdict as to the length of his life.

But the thought of death could not worry Hans. He had lived too near to danger all his life to be afraid when it threatened him as an act of God rather than through the hand of man.

At times he was not sure that he would not welcome death. Only his desire to rescue a few more victims from the stranglehold of oppression kept him from sinking into a coma of loneliness and despair.

Hans Schaeffer was, without a doubt, one of the loneliest men in the world; moreover, his name was seldom spoken except with loathing and antagonism.

Even those whom he championed, those who had him to thank for benefits they would never have enjoyed without his partisanship, were ungrateful and unfriendly.

He spoke the truth completely, without reserve, and such men make enemies wherever they go; truth is a light which blinds all but a few.

His articles were saleable in the foreign Press so long as they did not concern the countries in which he was staying at the moment, and he did much harm to the prestige of Nazi-ism by declaiming against the concentration camps and the treatment of prisoners.

He was a strange personality, tormented by a sympathy for the underling, which to a certain extent made him unbalanced.

Could he have reasoned more and felt less, he would have been a greater man and perhaps more forceful, but he was always completely carried away by the cause of the moment, devoured by a flaming emotion which expressed itself in an eloquence which gained him the title of "the man with the voice of fire."

Those who heard him speak were at the time enraptured by him.

He would move a crowd of hundreds of people to tears, or to rebellion, by the dynamic force of his

own feelings, but when he was finished he had nothing with which to cement and unite to himself the
people he had attracted.

Hans would not temper his principles to the
wind of popular opinion; unyielding and obstinate,
he preferred to stand alone.

He had an amazing but characteristic resistance,
and, as Ion had rightly seen, a lack of imagination;
but he was growing old, and he found it increasingly
difficult to keep confident and strong when all round
him there was fear, weakness, and indecision.

His supporters grew fewer, and every month it
became more difficult to distribute any of his articles
or leaflets in Germany.

Not many men were willing to take the risk of
being connected with him. There were punishments
for those who read his writings, death for those who
espoused his cause, and a price had been set on his
head.

Hans stood alone in the dark room, knowing himself to be an old man. It seemed to him, looking back,
that he had experienced few pleasures and much suffering in his life.

He remembered those whom he had trusted,
and with the memories came the pain of knowing
that most of them had betrayed him.

In all his friendships, sooner or later there had
come a parting of the ways, a moment when to his
companions had come the choice of loyalty or treach-
ery. Fear had invariably forced them to the latter.

Hans had journeyed on alone, too proud to com-
plain, conscious only of an aching loneliness, which
had grown greater until now it was almost a physical
agony.

Slowly he undressed, folding his clothes neatly
and precisely, hanging his coat over the back of a

chair, and then just before he got into bed he put out his hand and touched the case of his violin, and a faint smile drove the sadness from his mouth.

They had liked his playing; and that little sister of Ion's had listened to him with glowing eyes. He thought of her before finally sleep came to him.

*   *   *

Farther along the passage, Pamela could not sleep. She lay in the unfamiliar bed, thinking over the conversation which had taken place after supper had ended, and continuing it in her own mind as people often do when they are tired, or when their brain is stimulated to unusual activity.

Ion had been arguing with Hans again. There was a great affection between the two men, which showed itself in continued disagreement, in arguments which they enjoyed and over which they both became hotly vehement, striving as though it were a point of honour not to be defeated by the other.

Pamela was surprised to find how closely Ion had followed politics all over Europe in the past few years.

She learnt that he had been to Germany and Italy, and it was when they were going up to bed that Lisette had told her that in Paris they had often had dinner at a little restaurant where junior members of the Embassy and minor diplomats of all countries gathered.

Ion had been popular amongst them and he was able, through such friendships, to keep in touch with developments in his own country.

"At first I thought it strange," Lisette had confessed. "I had known many artists and even poets before, but not one who combined his artistry with an interest in practical affairs."

"That comes of being Scottish," Pamela had said with a smile. "Their reputation of being both fey and sharp in business is exaggerated but justly earned."

And then, on an impulse, as she reached her bed-room door she had kissed Lisette good-night.

"I have been so happy this evening," she had said. "I am glad I came."

Pamela's reminiscences of the evening were interrupted by a continually banging door.

At first the sound of it hardly penetrated her consciousness, and then gradually her attention was drawn to it to the exclusion of all else, so that it became an annoyance, an irritation from which she could not escape into thought.

Hoping that someone would go and close it, she found herself listening for the creak of the boards under a footstep, pretending that each bang was the final one, until she could bear it no longer.

Getting up, she put on the light cotton dressing-gown which lay across the foot of the bed, slipped her feet into slippers, raised the lighted candle high in her hand, and went to investigate.

The whole house was in darkness and her candle cast a golden light before her, making the retreating shadows seem mysterious and ominous as they encroached upon the radius of the candlelight.

It was a door on the ground floor, she decided, and she turned to the top of the stairs. Then, as she stood there, the door slammed again, this time sharply, and she heard someone approach.

She hesitated, and was just about to return to her room, when a voice below startled her.

"Stand still," it said. "Don't move! You are beautiful like that—whoever you may be."

*   *   *

If her first meeting with Gerald Durrant was unconventional, Pamela was to find in the days that followed that it was not more surprising than he was himself.

As she had stood at the top of the staircase, with the candle in her right hand, held level with her hair, so that it illuminated her face and shoulders, making her night-clothes seem like robes, she had been conscious that she excited him.

Excited not only in admiration but in a sort of fever, as if he were afraid that the picture he visualised would escape him.

Beauty was not the only thing, as Pamela was to learn, that had this strange power to excite Gerald.

It took her some time to learn anything about him, for, like many people who are eccentric in their appearance and behaviour, he had a deep and almost impenetrable reserve.

The next morning, when she told Lisette and Ion of her adventure, and how a strange man who exclaimed over her appearance had insisted on her standing there for several minutes before finally she fled in embarrassment back to the security of her room, they laughed.

"That is so like Gerald!" Ion exclaimed. "But I don't suppose the picture will ever materialise."

"I thought he must be an artist," Pamela said. "But who is he?"

"Gerald Durrant," Ion answered.

Then, as she looked vague, he added:

"Don't say you have never heard of him! My God, Pamela, what have you been doing with yourself all these years?"

"The name seems familiar," she said apologetically, "but I have never seen any of his work. Is he very important?"

"Of course he is," Ion replied. "He is one of the most criticised and yet one of the most successful of the younger artists of today. Oh, you won't find him hanging in the Academy, but he had an exhibition in the Leicester Square Galleries three years ago, and you have never seen anything like his notices.

"I read them before he chucked them into the fire without even looking at them. He hates showing his work, and generally the only way his agent can manage to obtain it is to come round in a car when Gerald is out and steal his paintings from the studio."

"Do you really think he will do a picture of me?" Pamela asked, rather flattered at the idea.

"Not a hope!" Ion answered rudely. "He goes wild, plans the picture in his mind, in some cases even starts on the canvass, and then scraps the whole idea for the next object which attracts his attention."

"But he may," Lisette said encouragingly. "One never knows with Gerald. Ion's bitter. He has started nearly half a dozen portraits of him and never completed one of them. But he finished mine."

"There was not much of you to be seen," Ion said. "Only the back of your head, the tip of your ear, and a great deal of my attic."

Lisette made a grimace.

"Never mind," she said. "The tip of my ear will go down to posterity, and, as you won't even be photographed, the future generations, when they are forced to read your books—as classics, of course—will have to imagine you."

"*Touché!*" Ion said. "You are quite right and I am wrong. Gerald shall paint a masterpiece of Pamela in her nightgown, carrying a candle, and call it 'The Lady of the Lamp,' and we will hang it over the mantelpiece at Glenferry when I come to my estate."

"Has he got any of his pictures here?" Pamela asked, ignoring all this badinage.

"I shouldn't think so," Ion answered, "although I really don't know. None of us are allowed into what he calls his studio. It is a small, disused lighthouse not far down the road, a perfect place for work, and I should have liked it myself.

"But Gerald is a bloated plutocrat, while Lisette and I are starving—in spite of my genius!

"Never mind, darling," he added to Lisette, who, having finished her breakfast, was knitting as usual. "Poor we may be, but we keep our souls, don't we?"

"We shall not keep anything," Lisette said quietly, "if you sit here talking all the morning."

"You are right again," Ion said with a sigh. "It's a disease."

Dropping a kiss on the back of her neck as he passed, he strolled towards the little hut among the trees.

"Do you really mean to say," Pamela asked when he was out of earshot, "that Ion works seriously every morning?"

"He tries to work," Lisette answered. "He cannot always do it, of course, but he stays in his hut with pencil and paper before him, and if he is unsuccessful he comes back punctually to lunch, generally in a very bad temper; but if the spirit moves him he stays on, so I take him food, like I did yesterday, much later in the afternoon."

"I am surprised," Pamela said. "I thought all authors had to wait for the Muse."

"That is a lot of nonsense invented by those who are lazy," Lisette replied. "The Muse is not likely to come while you are sitting chattering or amusing yourself in the company of other people, but if you are quiet and alone she may speak."

"Rather like the voice of God," Pamela said ruminatively.

"Isn't it much the same thing?" Lisette said surprisingly. "When Ion is really inspired, he is like someone who has seen a vision."

"He is," Pamela agreed, thinking of the moment on the river long ago, and of other instances in his childhood.

She had thought that she would be shy when she met Gerald Durrant again, but he had come striding into the garden when they were all seated at supper, and had dragged them away from their food to see a hedgehogs' nest about two or three hundred yards down the road.

He was very tall, with a thin and cadaverous face and heavy, dark eye-brows over deep blue eyes.

He wore a sweater trimmed with old Etonian colours, green corduroy trousers, and the loose tweed coat beloved of all Englishmen.

On his head was what had once been a green Tyrolean hat but which had long since lost its shape and colour, and on his feet were white rubber sandals of the type which are sold along the quays and in the market-places of every small provincial French town.

He was accompanied by two dogs. One was a mongrel which he had rescued from its owner, who after a bout of drunkenness had kicked it and broken a rib.

The other was a sentimental black spaniel of very doubtful pedigree, which never left his side for a moment and which watched him with adoring brown eyes as he sat and ate.

Ion was not with them. His work was obviously going well, for he had not appeared since breakfast, and Lisette fully expected that he would stay in the hut far into the night.

She had taken him over some food at about four o'clock, and he had cursed her for interrupting him, so after that she had left him severely alone, only placing a large jug of fresh water outside the door in case he should need it.

When Hans, Pamela, and Lisette had returned from watching the activities of the hedgehogs, and the small crowd of curious locals who followed them had dispersed, surprised at the interest strangers took in what was to them a familiar sight, they reseated themselves at supper.

When it was finished, Gerald rose from his seat and invited Pamela to walk with him down to the shore.

She accepted, secretly rather pleased, and they moved away together, talking at first in a rather constrained way, Pamela shy, Gerald somewhat taciturn, until finally, in a common interest—the love of animals—all their constraint and embarrassment vanished.

Every evening Gerald suggested a walk, and, as the others were too lazy, Pamela found herself getting to know and like this strange man.

On the evening of their fourth walk, as they were coming home, it was already dark and the bats swooping from the trees over the narrow roadway made Pamela wince and start apprehensively for fear that they should become entangled in her hair.

Gerald halted before they reached the village, and, putting his hands on her shoulders, he turned her round to face him.

They seemed to be utterly alone in a world of purple shadows; the pine trees towering tall and dark on one side of them and on the other a hedgerow fragrant with the second flowering of sweet honeysuckle shut out all visibility.

Pamela was conscious of the dry, dusty road beneath her feet, of the waves on the shore, of the gentle breeze that touched her hair, and of Gerald, tall, strangely magnetic, towering above her.

The strength of his hands holding her shoulders made her heart move in a quick anticipation.

"Look at me," he said, and his deep voice was vibrant.

She obeyed, and as she looked towards him, striving in the faint light to see the expression in his eyes, he gathered her into his arms and she felt his mouth seeking hers.

He kissed her fiercely, almost violently, and she was too surprised and dazed to repulse him; when he let her go she had to steady herself, gasping a little for breath.

Then without a word they walked on. Her thoughts were chaotic, and while she knew that she had not disliked Gerald's kisses she had been afraid of them.

He spoke no word of love, and the silence was unbroken save by the sound of their feet moving on the roadway.

Woman-like, she wanted him to talk of her, to hear him say he loved her, and yet she could not find words to begin a conversation; for she was still shy of the man who walked beside her, because she did not understand him.

As they drew near to the Inn they could hear the gentle strains of a violin. Instinctively Pamela's hands went to her hair, and then once again Gerald halted.

Beyond them lay the Inn; to the right, over the sand-dunes, lay the deserted lighthouse which Gerald had made his own.

He gripped her arm above the elbow with his

thin, strong fingers. There was a question in his silence, but as she did not speak he said:

"I want you, Pamela."

She could not mistake his meaning, and she was too wise to pretend an innocence or an ignorance of his desire.

She did not answer, and as if he sensed within her, not so much a refusal as a hesitation, he bent once again and kissed her, this time gently and without the passion and strength which had bruised her mouth before.

"Think it over, my sweet," he said.

Then he turned and walked away alone, the two dogs following at his heels.

Pamela stood looking after him until his tall figure finally vanished into the darkness and she could see him no more.

She would not have let him leave her so abruptly had she not feared that if she obeyed her instinct and stopped him, he might misunderstand her need of his presence.

His very casualness intrigued her, and even while she told herself that she should instantly dismiss the whole occurrence from her mind as another artistic eccentricity, she was honest enough to know that she could not help thinking of him until they met again.

She did not feel shocked at what he had suggested. It was perhaps an original manner of approach, which might be expected of him.

"What do I feel about Gerald?" she asked herself as she walked towards the Inn, and she could not answer her own question.

There was about him, she thought, the glamour both of a strong personality and of an artist—a mixture which appealed to and excited her.

Here was someone who fitted in well, she thought, with that new inner freedom which she was striving to attain; yet she knew that the unusual and unfamiliar was always a trap for the unwary, and because Gerald was unlike other men it did not make him the right man for her.

She was silent when she finally joined the group seated round Hans as he played. Sometimes they hummed, sometimes they sang, but mostly they listened in silence, all deep in their own thoughts and the visions that music conjures up.

Finally the bar closed for the night, and the proprietress wandered between the tables, tipping up the green wooden chairs in case of rain, before, with smiling *"bon-soirs"* which were almost blessings, she went to bed.

Lisette and Ion went indoors; only Pamela and Hans were left, and he was polishing and tending his violin before he laid it in its battered black leather case.

"You are worried?" he asked at length, as Pamela sat watching him.

Pamela shook her head.

"Not really," she answered. "I was thinking that sometimes it is difficult in life to know what is right and what is wrong—not ethical principles, but as regards oneself, one's own actions."

"The problem for nearly all of us," Hans replied, "is not right or wrong but laziness or action."

"Must one always choose?" Pamela asked.

"Is there such a thing as standing still?" he questioned. "I doubt it."

He looked at her with kindly eyes, as if he guessed what her troubles were but was too tactful to refer to them.

Instead he took up his violin again and played

very softly, for her alone, the "In Spring" of Schubert. The passionate, ringing prayer which at the same time is pure and tender made Pamela feel that the love she sought must be all this and more.

Every great piece of music makes the listener believe that: just one note more and all knowledge and all truth will be theirs.

It leads the mind higher and higher, until it seems that the harmony must break through the confines of mind and matter, which hold the spirit earthbound, never quite free.

Pamela listened, followed by a vague sense of disappointment that it could not give her more, but when Hans had finished playing she knew that he had at the moment given her an answer to her question.

She knew now what she wanted. Whether Gerald could or could not supply it was a question for the future.

THE WISDOM OF THE LIGHT OF ASIA

Four higher roadways be. Only those feet
  May tread them which have done with earthly
    things,
Right Purity, Right Thought, Right Loneliness,
  Right Rapture. Spread no wings

For Sunward flight, thou soul with unplumed
  vans!
  Sweet is the lower air, and safe and known
The homely levels; only strong ones leave
  The nest each makes his own.

Dear is the love, I know, of Wife and Child;
  Pleasant the friends and pastimes of your
    years;
Fruitful of good Life's gentle charities;
  Firm-set, though false, its fears.

Live—ye who must—such lives as live on these;
Make golden stairways of your weaknesses; rise
By daily sojourn with those phantasies
  To lovelier verities.

So shall ye pass to clearer heights and find
  Easier ascents and lighter loads of sins,
And larger will to burst the bonds of sense,
  Entering the PATH.

—*Bhagavad-Gita*

Chapter Five

Gerald thrust open the door of his studio and entered into the darkness.

He was too familiar with the shape of the room and with its contents to have to grope his way, and he moved easily to where he knew he would find matches to light the heavy oil-lamps which swung from the ceiling on chains.

He had not looked back when he had left Pamela standing staring after him; he knew that she would not follow, and he imagined her walking slowly on towards the Inn, her thoughts still with him.

He pulled down the lamp, the chains from which it was suspended squeaked and groaned their need of oil, and then the yellow flame lit the circular room with that warm, mellow beauty of candlelight.

The ceiling, which had once divided the old lighthouse into two rooms, had been removed, and now the whole building consisted of one tower, its height out of all proportion to its breadth, and yet in some quaint way it was beautiful.

At the very top of the tower there were the circular windows through which at one time a light had flashed out to sea.

Large windows had been built in what had been the downstairs room, and Gerald had widened them still farther.

Leading out of the tower were two or three ram-shackle rooms which were seldom used, for he pre-ferred to live at the Inn, allowing his studio to be en-tered by a cleaner only when he himself was absent from Bugalé.

Even his closest friends were not invited inside his place of work, which was littered with paint-rags, torn-up drawings, brushes, a discarded canvass or two, and bones which the dogs had brought in.

On a ledge round the walls were various pictures. Some of them were finished, others were canvasses with only a line or two scrawled on them or the out-line of a figure visible in a *mêlée* of colours, which suggested work executed on the spur of inspiration of the moment and never completed.

On the easel stood a portrait of Pamela; the charcoal outline of the body was complete, but the face, though in paint, was but half-finished.

Gerald stood back and looked at it, frowning in concentration.

It was easy to see why his work was successful, for every picture in the room had that strange, arrest-ing quality of strength which proclaims the artist who has mastered his technique and added to it some genius of his own.

There was some other quality too which showed in every one of his pictures and most forcibly in the one he had begun of Pamela.

There was a bitterness, a brutality, underlying the colour and the sense of light for which he was famous.

It was as if the cynicism of the artist's mind was shown in the loveliness of sky and sea or the gentle unfolding of a tree in spring.

In his portraits this peculiarity was startling.

He had drawn Pamela as he first saw her standing on the top of the stairs, holding the lighted candle.

He had captured the look of startled surprise, and of youth and elasticity, but at the same time he had inserted into the picture something of himself, which made the lines of her body, revealed through the transparency of her nightgown, falsely suggestive.

In the expression of her face, too, revealed by the candle, there was almost an invitation.

The picture gave one the impression of holding a deep meaning, yet one which could be easily attributed to a commonplace explanation. The deep shadows, as yet briefly sketched in, were menacing.

Gerald had in fact portrayed a girl with Pamela's face, on some secret errand, seeking perhaps the room of her lover or keeping a clandestine tryst.

He had the capacity for conveying with a few lines of his pencil or brush as much as another man might write in a dozen pages of a book.

There was personality and brilliance in every one of his pictures, and yet each and all were tainted in the same way, so that no-one felt inclined to exclaim "How beautiful!" but instead everything he did was "interesting," or "astonishing."

Particularly in his pictures of women this curious characteristic was most obvious.

One of the pictures propped against the wall was of a nude girl, with red hair, reclining on a dark rug, her back to the artist, her face turned so that only the curve of her cheek was visible, and the lovely lines of jaw and neck.

A conventional pose, yet Gerald had invested it with something new. The girl was recumbent but not reposeful. She seemed to be listening, every muscle taut so that at any moment she could spring into action.

There was something almost sinister in the naked figure whose stillness was so superficial. For what was she waiting? For whom?

There was a restlessness in the picture which affected even the most phlegmatic spectator.

Gerald stood still in the centre of the room, his dogs watching him. He picked up a brush and a palette from where they stood ready beside the easel, yet when they were in his hands he hesitated.

He stared at the picture as if aware that something was wrong, but he was powerless for the moment to see where the fault lay.

The light of the lamp above threw dark shadows beneath his thick eye-brows and accentuated the lines from nose to mouth, so that the bitterness of the pictures was echoed in their artist's face.

It was a face of supreme disillusionment, and its cadaverous look was almost fanatical.

Thirty-eight years ago Gerald Durrant had been born of a conventional country family, with the tradition of many generations of ancestors whose names figured prominently in the history of the Army and the Navy.

Gerald's father had served for many years in the Brigade of Guards, until, on the death of his father, he inherited a considerable fortune and the old Manor House which had been the home of the family since its foundation.

He married the youngest daughter of a North Country peer who shared his sporting tastes.

Their eldest son was a delight to them both, but they accepted him calmly and without undue expression, feeling that it was fit and right that the Durrant family should, as it always had, produce boys to follow in the footsteps of the past.

By the time Gerald was nine he had three brothers and a sister. It was on his tenth birthday that an incident took place which changed his character, so that later he grew utterly alien to his family and his breeding.

Brought up among animals, he had in the first years of his life taken as his particular pet one of his father's retrievers.

Gradually the dog, which seldom left the small boy's side and which slept at the foot of his bed, became known as "Master Gerald's," and Rex, as he was called, enjoyed a less strenuous but less sporting life in consequence.

The dog grew older and perhaps the lazy life disagreed with his health, for he became disagreeable with age, and, although always adoring and gentle wtih Gerald, he was increasingly ferocious and uncertain where strangers or the other children were concerned.

Gerald could do anything with him, and Rex obeyed him implicitly, but Gerald was not always there; his education had started at a preparatory boarding-school.

He enjoyed his first term. He had an ingenuous charm which made him popular with boys of his own age, he was intelligent and interested in his lessons, and the school-masters found him a pleasing pupil.

He returned home delighted that the holidays had come and with none of that dread of next term which so often overshadows a small boy's happiness.

The car met him at the station and he chattered to the chauffeur on the way, planning all sorts of excitements and mentioning Rex continually and the ecstatic welcome he expected from him.

When he ran up the broad steps to kiss his mother affectionately in the hall, his first question was for his dog.

"Where is Rex, Mother?" he asked. "Why isn't he here?"

Lady Durrant put out her hand and laid it on her small son's shoulder.

"I am sorry, Gerald," she said gently, "but I have bad news for you."

Gerald's face whitened, and in his eyes, staring up at her, there was an agony of apprehension.

"Rex," she continued, "was old—you know that, Gerald—and when you went away we couldn't manage him. He flew at the servants and it wasn't safe for Mary. She is very little, you see—not yet three —and he might have injured her. So we had him put to sleep, dear; it was the only thing to do."

"You killed him?" Gerald exclaimed, and his mother was startled by the pain in his voice.

He did not cry, but she saw the knuckles whiten on his small hands as he clenched them.

"I hate you!" he said quietly and intensely, and before she could say anything else he turned and left her.

Gerald was quiet during those holidays. He did not again refer to his dog, and Lady Durrant hoped that he would forget.

His father offered him another retriever but he refused, without explanation, and they thought it best to leave the boy alone, thinking that by the next holidays he would be only too glad to have a puppy to train from a spring litter.

Lady Durrant was an unimaginative woman. She was fond of her children, but they occupied only a part of her life.

She enjoyed the companionship of her husband

and the advantages of his position, and she had a number of duties on the estate and in the county which kept her busy throughout the year.

She hardly noticed that her eldest son was avoiding her, and if she sometimes questioned his reserve she was not seriously perturbed, for she thought it bad for boys to be unduly demonstrative, and she treated her sons with a frank and easy comradeship which paid little account to their age.

But Gerald's hatred of his mother was to poison his entire existence.

He grew moody and his health suffered, for he would lie awake at night brooding over his dog's death, convinced that he had failed the animal in its hour of need, and torturing himself, with all the powerful imagination of a child, with the thought that Rex had suffered.

It would have been far better if he could have spoken of what he felt, if he had been encouraged to discuss his misery. Instead, it was a canker growing within him, spreading until it tainted his entire being.

Only when it was far too late did Lady Durrant begin to wonder how she and her husband could have produced this strange, sullen child, who seemed to have little in common with his cheerful, ordinary brothers.

An attitude of mind, once deeply implanted, gradually submerges the whole character. As Gerald grew older he of course partially forgot Rex—or at any rate he did not think of him—but the hatred of his mother remained.

Through this obsession he viewed the whole world, finding it bitter and being ever on the defensive against happiness.

He startled his parents by refusing to contemplate a career in either the Army or the Navy.

He left his school, where he had made few friends but gained the unqualified dislike of the masters, who found him lazy and impudent, with a rudeness which came not from high spirits but from some detached disdain which they could not understand or destroy.

At nineteen Gerald had already begun to experiment, in a desultory way, at painting.

He was not very successful, veering towards the futuristic school, conscious that there was within himself a desire to portray in some bold, colourful manner his own suppressed personality.

He had found at school that he had a trick of seeing people in a distorted fashion which at first seemed comical. When he was not lazy he would sketch swiftly in a few clever strokes a portrait of some master or visitor to the school.

His companions would applaud or laugh at his efforts, at the same time whispering that there was something "rather beastly in the way Durrant sees things," which made him no more popular with them.

He withstood the onslaught of both his parents to force him to choose a career, and spent two or three years leisurely moving from London to the country and back again.

They were powerless to compel him to work, for his grandmother had left him, on her death, a small but adequate income.

They complained, argued, and at last begged him to make up his mind on some occupation, but when he finally announced that he had decided to become an artist, his father's rage was uncontrollable.

His fury and his frequent letters on a "lazy, good-for-nothing existence" had no effect on Gerald, who, without replying, departed to study in Paris.

It was a year later, when he had come home for

a brief holiday, that the episode took place which was to set the seal on what was already a twisted and tortured mind.

He had, in contradistinction to his dislike of his mother, a strange shyness which was almost reverence for other women. He knew few girls, for his sister was younger than himself and her friends were still in the school-room.

In Paris, as in London, he had avoided women and had been chaffed by his companions, who called him a woman-hater.

As it happened, the affection in his nature, frustrated by his unnatural childhood, had made him, if anything, an idealist.

All else in his life was coloured and distorted by the bitterness with which he faced everyday existence, but where women were concerned, because they were an unknown quantity, Gerald approached them with awe and an old-fashioned chivalry.

Disliking athletics, without the experience of hero-worship, and finding no solace in religion, Gerald —because every man must worship at some altar— vowed his allegiance to chastity until the woman whom he loved should release him from his vows.

It was a secret that he treasured within himself, strengthened by resolution year by year until it grew into an obsession.

Other women, however seductive, were no temptation while he was spiritually as well as physically in search of the woman he would love and marry.

When he was twenty-two he met her.

She was small and exquisite, and they were introduced at a cocktail-party given by a successful stage designer who had invited Gerald at the last moment on meeting him casually in Piccadilly.

Disliking parties, Gerald had repressed the inclination to leave as soon as he arrived only out of consideration for his host, whom he admired for having, by unusual and original ideas of stage decor, attracted the attention of the whole artistic world.

Casually a man he had known at Eton hailed him, asked him a few commonplace questions, introduced his companion, and moved away into the crowd.

For years afterwards Gerald was to remember the curious, tight feeling which constricted his chest, the lump in his throat, and the words which he could not utter when he found himself staring into Mona's face.

Her loveliness, her smallness, and the fastidious manner in which she moved and spoke, fascinated him so that he walked the streets all that night, knowing himself to be crazily in love.

It was a love which was like a dam breaking, for the reserve of years was swept away by a wildness and extravagance of emotion which transformed him, made him a stranger to himself.

He wanted to give her the moon, the stars, the earth, and everything he saw and knew of, which for the first time since childhood seemed to him beautiful. Cynicism had gone from him.

Mona accepted his incoherent passion as she finally accepted his proposal of marriage, with a calm detachment which entranced him and brought him to his knees in gratitude.

They were married at St. Margaret's, Westminster. Gerald had protested, begged for a quiet wedding, but his desires were swept aside, for Mona wanted a fashionable beginning to her married life.

She was older than Gerald by three years, and he did not know, and there was no-one to tell him, that she had begun to be afraid of losing the publicity and Press notices which were as the breath of life to her.

The eldest son and heir to one of the oldest families in England was all she had hoped for in a husband.

Although she found Gerald rather strange and unconventional, she had confidence in her own power to alter him after marriage.

His parents also were pleased; Gerald's income was augmented with a large settlement from his father, and he received from his mother, for the first time in many years, an expression of satisfaction.

He realised that they all thought he would settle down now and behave in what they considered to be a normal way of living, but he was too much in love to worry about the future.

He was counting the days until Mona should be his, and in his imagination he worshipped her as if she were some saint who had condescended to an earthly union.

When he entered her bed-room on their wedding-night in the overheated and super-luxurious Hotel in which Mona had chosen to begin their honeymoon, he walked as a man dazed and bewildered by the glory that is upon him.

Mona was in bed, her fair hair curled round her head like a tiny halo, the soft lace of her nightgown revealing her white arms and shoulders.

He stood staring at her for a long time, and then when she questioned his silence he tried in inarticulate and broken words to tell her something of the love he felt for her.

Hesitatingly, with the embarrassment of a sincerity which is naked because it comes from the very depths of a man's being, he told her how he had remained through his life immaculate for this moment.

It was a confession which was to close in finality his past and open the doors to the glorious fulfilment of which he had dreamed for years.

He paused, his burning eyes searching her face for an echo of the wonder he felt surging within himself.

Then Mona sniggered.

It was the almost unconscious action of a girl faced by something unexpected which she did not understand, vaguely resented, and more certainly disliked.

Gerald revealing his soul seemed to her indecent, and, brought up to distrust all emotion except that which was superficial, her embarrassment relieved itself in a sound half of laughter and half of incredulity.

If she had struck him in the face or stabbed him, Gerald could not have been more surprised.

He stared at her, hardly understanding what had happened, yet feeling as if an icy hand had laid itself upon him.

"Do you really mean to say," Mona asked in almost a shocked tone, "that you have never slept with a woman?"

A terrible fear and suspicion came to Gerald. He gripped her arms.

"Why are you so surprised?" he asked. "And why did you laugh just now? You weren't amused, you weren't even disdainful, you were ... ashamed. Why?"

"Let me go," Mona said, twisting ineffectually in his grasp. "How dare you try to bully me! I don't know what you mean."

"Answer me," Gerald said fiercely. "Why are you afraid?"

When she did not answer, he put his hand under her chin and forced her face up to his.

"Have you ever lived with a man before?"

He read the answer in her eyes, which could not meet his, in the sudden movement as she tried to shrink away from him, and in the ineffective, untruthful words which came unconvincingly to her lips.

Then Gerald lost all control. Twice he struck her, and when she screamed and lay moaning, a huddled mass of tears and abuse, he left the room.

Ten minutes later he had left the Hotel. He spent the night drinking and awoke at noon the next day in the bed-room of a prostitute he had picked up on the streets.

After paying her lavishly for her services, he had taken an aeroplane to Paris and returned to his studio in the Latin Quarter.

He had never seen his wife again. Through his solicitors he had sent her evidence for divorce, and had refused to answer or even read the letters his parents had written to him.

From that time on there was no likelihood of his friends accusing him of being a woman-hater, for there were always women in his life, and their taunts of past years were at last fully justified.

Only with time came a certain mellowing in that he enjoyed his work, though he despised the success it brought him.

He found happiness, too, in the companionship of his dogs, and while women came and went in his life, to the dogs he was faithful, giving them all the affection that was left in his nature.

Beauty still elated him, but a diabolical bitterness crept into eveything he did. He knew it and gloried in it.

But, staring now at the portrait of Pamela, he realised how far he had strayed from the truth; the picture was not what he had seen as she had stood hesitant and startled on the stairs so that he had cried out at her.

Picking up a palette-knife, Gerald scraped the paint from the canvass, and then, beholding the smudged mess which was all that was left of many hours' work ,he sighed deeply and covered his tired eyes with his hands.

For the first time in many years he began to doubt himself.

*   *   *

It was a misty, grey day. The sea, sky, and stone Church, and the trees, the fields, and the empty sands, seemed to be tinged with a silver melancholy, and Pamela, taking a morning walk along the dunes, was conscious that she was depressed.

For the first time since her arrival in Bugalé she felt lonely, and although she accused herself of being unreasonable, she could not throw off the cloud which seemed to encompass her mind without regard of sense or logic.

All women are creatures of moods; Pamela was no exception, and today she felt isolated, even alien to the little community of which she was now an acknowledged part.

Perhaps it was her lack of occupation, when they were all busy and intent on their own interests, which made the hours she spent alone seem at times a penance.

But today was somewhat exceptional; Ion had worked all night and now was sleeping or resting, but he required Lisette's presence beside him.

Hans was not to be found, and after breakfast

Gerald had gone to his studio, leaving Pamela with a question to which she must find an answer before evening.

He had suggested that he should paint a portrait of her.

He had spoken of it the night before, when Ion and Lisette were present, and their assumption that Pamela would accept such an offer with delight made her check the refusal which came spontaneously to her lips.

"I thought of a picture on the stairs as I first saw you with a candle in your hand," Gerald had said, "but I have changed my mind. There is something about both you and Ion which belongs to the open air, and I want an atmosphere of sea and sky, a sense of wild enchantment."

"You are right," Liestte said, "although I never noticed it before. Perhaps that is why Ion is different from all the other writers I have known."

"You have never known one who was worth a damn," Ion interposed.

Lisette gave him a mocking smile as if challenging his conceit, then she said:

"Perhaps that is the big difference between a true artist and an imitative one."

"You mean that the true artist must draw his inspiration from nature?" Pamela asked.

"Not his inspiration," said Ion, who could never resist taking part in any argument, whatever it was about, "but his breath of life, the impetus by which he lives and has his being! Nature must be revealed to him, must receive and sustain him! He can give and create only from himself—as a jug pours out its contents, so does an artist."

"I think a greyness," Gerald went on, ignoring the conversation, "with behind it a hint of sunlight which will sooner or later break through the clouds. There is an uncertainty about Pamela—suspended between heaven and earth, she cannot make up her mind to accept either."

Pamela had been surprised at his words, and she thought of them now as she walked along the shore.

That hint of sunlight which Gerald had seen above her—surely it was symbolic of what not only she but everyone else hoped for, believed in, and anticipated, but which tantalisingly withheld itself.

The sunshine of luck, good fortune, love, and happiness remained clouded, unrevealed, leaving for so many people a life of all-pervading greyness.

She sat down to windward of a large rock, looking out to sea and trying not to concentrate on her thoughts but to let them ripple through her mind unuttered and half-formulated, rising and falling like the waves.

There was a restlessness within her, a desire for what she neither knew nor felt but sensed as a person will sense the presence of another in a dark room.

'Is there no contentment for me?' she thought.

She questioned her own ingratitude, the contrast between her life in England and her life here in Bugalé standing parallel in her mind for comparison, then she turned her head to see Arthur standing a little way apart, in the act of descending to the beach.

She was not surprised to see him, for Arthur could never amaze or astonish her whatever he did, but she was genuinely glad.

Rising to her feet, she ran to greet him with the spontaneous, unconcealed joy that a small girl might show when a favourite relative visits her at school.

Arthur, with his well-cut grey suit, his quiet, steady manner, and his companionable smile, was the one person she wanted at this particular moment.

She was to remember how she thought, that night when she touched his hands, that Arthur was like a harbour into which a ship could sail battered and weary from the rough seas.

Wherever the ship might be, in whatever corner of the globe, the harbour would remain, its protection unchanging.

"How did you find me?" Pamela asked.

"They told me at the Inn that you had gone for a walk," he said, as if she referred to this present moment. "Does one ever walk at the seaside except on the shore?"

Pamela laughed.

"How sensible you are!" she said. "I should have sat down disconsolately and waited."

"So should I if I had not found you," Arthur said gently.

Then, as if to hide the purpose which she might fathom behind his remark, he asked, "Did you get here all right? I was worried in case you had no money."

"I had some," she said with a smile, "but it was kind of you to worry about it."

He looked relieved, and she asked:

"Were your family very angry with me?"

"They were surprised," Arthur answered.

There was a suspicion of a twinkle in his eye, as though he recalled their amazement and saw the humour of it.

"I am sorry," Pamela said. "I had to go. You understood, didn't you?"

"I will try to understand," Arthur said gently, "if you will tell me why."

"I read Ion's book The Forgotten City," Pamela said, clasping her hands together as she spoke.

She raised her head and looked out to sea. She

might have been a schoolgirl reciting a lesson to someone in authority.

She appeared very young at that moment as the wind caught her hair and blew it round her forehead and cheeks; and in order to pay attention to her words, Arthur steeled himself against a tenderness which invaded him.

"I read on and on until I finished it. Have you read it, Arthur?"

"Yes," he said.

He did not add that he had searched each page, each word, for some clue to what had driven her, without forethought or plan, to seek her brother.

"Then perhaps you can understand," Pamela said. "Or perhaps the story did not have the same effect on you. It seemed to open a window within me which had been closed.

"I saw that I had been shut in, that I had let myself forget everything I had once known—everything true, real, and beautiful which had been mine years ago with Ion at Glenferry.

"And the love of the Abbot John and Donna Christina made me think that within each of us there is a City which is forgotten. That night I began to remember, and in remembering I knew I must start again, for nothing else is of consequence except that I should find again all I once loved.

"So I came away, because I felt suffocated by all that was familiar and because I knew I must find Ion."

She finished speaking and turned to look at Arthur. She had spoken in low, level tones, without emphasis or hesitation but with a sincerity which made each of her sentences convey more than the meaning of her words.

"And has Ion been able to help you?" Arthur asked.

Pamela seemed for a moment startled by his question.

"I don't know," she said, then added in doubtful explanation, "It has been wonderful to see him again, and his friends here are so interesting. I have enjoyed every moment since I arrived."

"And how long do you intend to stay?" he asked.

"I haven't thought," Pamela confessed. "Honestly, Arthur, I haven't even begun to plan or face the future. I only knew that night in your home that something tremendous had happened to me, and that I must run away from everything and everybody to try to find . . ."

She hesitated, then ended: "Myself."

"I see," Arthur said reflectively, as if he did not yet understand but was still struggling to follow her thoughts and actions with comprehension and sympathy.

He pulled out his pipe from his pocket and started to fill it.

'How nice he is!' Pamela thought.

He had not reproached her by word or inference for what must have been to him a cruel surprise, to be followed by an awkward explanation to his parents.

The strange thought came to her that Arthur was linked in her imaginings of St. Joseph.

Just so reliable and strong, like a rock deep-grounded in the earth, incapable of the ecstasy of vision but instead filled with wisdom.

'St. Joseph must have held a deep joy within him,' she thought, 'to be the chosen protector of the Blessed Maid.'

He could accept, hold in security, and house the Universe, while the vastness of the miracle transcended and escaped his understanding; he was happy to serve those whom he loved in unquestioning obedience to his instinct.

And as posterity makes no hero of St. Joseph, so acquaintances thought of Arthur as a "dull dog," believing him to be a man without heights or depths.

Arthur saw and understood a great deal more than most people imagined of him, but words did not come easily to his lips, for they were but vehicles, and as such they could only carry him on a necessary journey from here to there.

"Let others talk," was his attitude, and when they had finished he was content to sort out in his own mind things thus acquired, to discard or to add to his convictions without the need of formal expression.

Humbly he compared himself—middle-aged, dull, and tongue-tied—to the brilliant, vivid beauty that he saw in the girl he loved, and he thought himself presumptuous to desire her.

Yet his sound commonsense told him that she needed someone like himself to balance and hold her steady in her own development.

He had known that he loved her within a few moments of their first meeting, but it had taken him two years of waiting for the right moment, and of gradually trying to gain her interest.

Impulse of any sort was unknown to Arthur. In everything he did there was the gradual observation of the subject, the contemplation with which he would encircle and slowly acquire a complete understanding of that which interested him.

Pamela's beauty drew and attracted him to her, but he desired not only that loveliness which, unconsciously, she gave by her very presence to all men and to the world, but also to discover the whole of her personality, as yet not fully developed.

Slowly but surely Arthur built up his comprehension of Pamela, adding to the foundation of his attraction to her, testing each conclusion to which he came until he was certain that it was true and sincere.

When he finally asked her to become his wife, he offered her not only a deep love and the adoration of a man whose nature made him find one woman who mattered in his life, but also an understanding deeper than knowledge and more intelligent than sympathy.

Arthur's interest in people started in 1918 when as a young subaltern he had been captured at the beginning of the year and interned in a prison-camp until the armistice.

He had been confined with over a hundred of his own countrymen, all of whom reacted in different ways to imprisonment.

Some—but these were few—accepted their life philosophically and passed the hours reading, or playing Patience or any other game which kept them from the necessity of inward thought.

Others fought nervously and irritably against their internment, wasting their energy and even their health in impotent rage which made neither their own fate nor the life of their companions any easier.

Hope was kept alive in many by fruitless anticipation of escape.

They would spend hours daily on plans which had not the slightest chance of success—a fact known to most of them, in the sincerity of their hearts. But such plotting served as a kind of drug to keep them from despair.

Arthur learnt in Germany that all men are alike in one particular: sooner or later they must seek a confessional, and if their confidence is not sought they will in their own good time speak of themselves to any sympathetic person who will listen.

A man who is silent inspires in those who meet him either a disdain or a desire for confidence, and to the men who were his fellow-prisoners Arthur became, young as he was, a listener on whom they could always rely for sympathetic attention.

The conversation at the prison camp was often of women. It would have been unnatural had a hundred men, mostly young and virile, not thought of sex. In a crowd, the conversation was frequently bawdy and often an irritant to their enforced chastity.

But when there was no audience, the same men who had talked glibly of brothels, of passionate interludes, and of sensuous embraces, would speak of their wives, their fiancées, or the girls they had once known, with tenderness and reverence.

It had taken Arthur a long time after the war to understand again the importance of trivialities.

In many of his contemporaries such restlessness expressed itself in wild instability, and they sought relief in dancing, women, drink, or any new experiment which presented itself at the moment.

Arthur could find no solace in any of these things.

For a time he stayed in the country, until the monotonous round of shooting, fishing, and visiting-guests drove him into his father's business.

But he found there that the work did not demand enough of him. It was too easy and too well-organised; he knew that if he did not arrive at ten o'clock in the morning, he would not be missed.

So he turned to something which was difficult, something which would employ his mind even as his friends sought to employ their bodies: he discovered books.

To everyone comes a moment when they find

for themselves the joy of what the world calls intellectuality but what is really the spirit's first hunger for truth.

Reading is like eating, a thing done almost unconsciously, until concentration on taste brings something similar to an epicurean satisfaction.

Books are an entertainment or a relief until suddenly, without warning, they open wide a new field of vision, and man becomes initiated.

It requires only a man's interest to lead him on, higher, to that capability of knowledge which lies within himself.

At first Arthur read as other men danced, as an escape, and then he read as a collector who searches the world over for some new specimen.

When he had first met Pamela's father, they had recognised each other with the freemasonry of scholars.

In the stuffy, tiny study which looked on to the dismal back-yard where the family washing was hung regularly every Monday, Arthur found a companionship he had never previously known.

He had been sitting in a leather arm-chair, his pipe between his teeth, his legs crossed, listening, absorbing, conscious of a deep peace, when the door opened.

Pamela stood there.

To Arthur at that moment she seemed the physical embodiment of everything beautiful which lay within the books that stretched all round her from floor to ceiling.

He felt the cool slimness of her hand in his, and for the first time in his life he knew within him the trembling of a flame too ecstatic for passion, yet containing in its springing everything that passion desires.

'Here is the companion of my dreams,' he thought, and the wonder of her gripped at his throat.

She had made him feel clumsy, as though she were a bird which he might bruise with rough hands; and looking at her now on the sands at Bugalé, he noticed again that bird-like quality about her.

Suddenly his heart was afraid, for had he not tried to cage her behind the golden bars of his home? He was so ashamed that his voice was humble when he said:

"I haven't come here to worry you, Pamela, only to reassure myself, but there is one thing I must do before I leave you, one thing which you must not refuse me."

"Which is . . . ?" Pamela asked.

"Allow me to leave you some money," Arthur said. "And when you have spent it, promise me that you will write for more. That is, if you haven't come home by that time."

"You don't mind giving it to me?" Pamela asked. "I'm running away from you, remember."

"Of course not," Arthur said in relief. "I was only afraid that you would refuse. As to your running away, will you allow that it is from your marriage which you have fled—not from me?"

Pamela put out her hand and touched his.

"Dearest and kindest Arthur," she said, "you are much too nice to me. I know I don't deserve it, and I know quite well what my mother and yours must think of me."

"Where you and I are concerned," Arthur said, "does it matter what anyone thinks? You want freedom and I want to help you. Surely that is all that matters."

"Do you think I am wrong?" Pamela questioned.

"Wrong?" Arthur said, frowning a little. "I don't

believe that you could do anything which was wrong for yourself, whatever it might seem to other people."

"Oh, don't trust me like that!" Pamela cried. "It frightens me."

"But why?" Arthur replied. "You know what you are trying to find, and while I cannot understand completely, I can at least do nothing to prevent or hamper you, and I can stop other people from interfering."

"But I want to know what you think," Pamela persisted.

"It is hard to put into words," Arthur said slowly. "I have always believed for myself that in doing the ordinary things of life to the best of one's ability, in time a man can discover that detachment which is, I think, what you mean by freedom.

"But I am an ordinary, humdrum sort of fellow, and for you to try to confine yourself within my bounds is neither possible nor probable."

'He is right,' Pamela thought. 'If the growth is within, environment should not matter.'

Aloud she said:

"Then you are stronger than I, for I am influenced and handicapped by my surroundings. 'Stone walls' do prove a prison for me. That is weak, Arthur, isn't it, and small?"

"You are neither," Arthur replied.

He raised her hand which still covered his to his lips, then rose to his feet and drew her up beside him.

"I am going now. I only came because I wanted to be certain of your safety."

"Oh, stay!" Pamela protested. "Stay for the night, or anyhow until the evening. I want you to meet Ion, and I want . . ."

She hesitated, not sure of what she did want, except suddenly she was aware that Arthur and Gerald should not meet. There was no particular reason why they should not, yet her instinct told her that they were utterly alien.

"No, I will catch the afternoon train," Arthur said. "There is a taxi waiting for me."

They walked together over the sands towards the Inn, Pamela holding on to his arm, and talking of many things while her mind, beneath its superficiality, thought of him.

It was best that he should go, but possessively she desired the comfort of his presence.

"Bless you, my dearest," he said in farewell, and she could not answer him.

His taxi moved away and she waited until it had turned the corner. She stood wondering why her sense of security must depart with him.

Arthur gave her confidence as if he were a scaffolding on which she depended for her safety, and in his absence she felt frail and uncertain.

THE WISDOM OF THE ELEUSINIAN MYSTERIES

There is a faculty of the human mind which is superior to all which is born or begotten. Through it we are enabled to attain union with the superior intelligences, to become transported beyond the scenes of this world, and to partake of the higher life and the peculiar powers of the Heavenly ones.

—Iamblichus

more experience trying to tell, which ones I ... stupid I have been. I did not understand ... that there was always an alternative."

And Pamela said:

"Now, how can you have any regrets ...

Chapter Six

The moon, almost full, shone over the sea, giving to each movement of the water a ripple of silver light and turning the long stretch of pale sand which bordered the waves into a ghost of its golden self.

Pamela stood alone a few yards from the waves as they crept, on their predestined course, slowly higher and higher up the sand.

She saw and felt the beauty that was all round her, yet it was subservient to her mind, which was troubled with other things.

For to each of us loveliness exists only in our power to absorb it.

We can remain unmoved as the sun lifts the misty veil of morning from the wonder of the Acropolis, just as we can submerge our whole being in the glory of a flower blooming in the window-box of an attic.

Pamela was experiencing war within herself, a revolution which, obstructing all expansion, divided her energy against itself, destroying her peace.

That afternoon she had begun to sit for Gerald, having finally decided that she would allow him to paint the portrait he desired.

On first entering his studio she had exclaimed at the strangeness of it, but the brightness from the many windows had dispelled her fears and alleviated her shyness.

Then he had drawn the curtains until the sunlight was diffused to a cool green light, as if she were submerged in water; the dome over her head was shrouded save for one small, uncovered pane, which lit her cheek and hair.

Gerald took a long time to pose her. He had arranged her first this way and then that, till at last he was satisfied, and she, seated on the model throne, leant against a collection of rugs draped to represent a rock, her face half-turned as if she were looking out to sea.

Gerald wore a dirty, blue, paint-stained overall which gave him the appearance of some character from a mediaeval play.

He worked fiercely, almost furiously, at his canvass, and he did not speak until the sharp pain of cramp in Pamela's neck made her ask for rest.

"Yes, yes," he said impatiently. "Get down—if you must."

She stretched her legs and arms in relief, then rose to look at what he had drawn; but he stopped her.

"Not now," he said. "I hate my work being seen until it is finished."

With a smile, she obeyed him without protest and instead moved away to inspect the other pictures placed round the walls.

Gerald lit a cigarette and stood there watching her.

"Why are you afraid?" he asked.

"I?" Pamela questioned.

"You are, aren't you?" Gerald went on. "Is it of me or of yourself?"

She did not answer. Walking across the room, he stood before her, forcing her by his will, but without

words, to look at him. Compelled, she raised her
eyes, and, held prisoner by what she saw in his, she
felt his arms encircle her body.

"I want you," he said, and kissed her lips.

"And you want me, too," he murmured, and with
his words released her mouth.

Pamela put out her hands and tried to move,
but he held her captive. She was trembling and a
pulse throbbing within her made her breath come
quickly.

She quivered as she spoke, her voice hardly
above a whisper.

"I don't... know, I don't know. Please... Gerald, let me ... go."

As if he would not force a decision upon her
yet, as abruptly as he had taken her he let her go.

After a minute Pamela moved back to the throne
and took up her pose again. Without comment, Gerald
started to work.

When it was five o'clock he boiled water in a ket-
tle on an oil-stove which stood in the small adjacent
kitchen, and he brought her the tea, adding to the
cup a slice of lemon, for there was no milk.

When they had drunk the tea and eaten some
small sweet biscuits, their rôles reversed, and Pamela
lost her shyness as Gerald started to tell her, hesitant-
ly, uneasily, as a man not used to confidences, about
his work.

She was interested, but intuitively she felt that
there must be some reason for his story, unexpected
and unsolicited; but, wisely, she waited, encouraging
him by her attention, and asking few questions, until he spoke of his marriage.

She then thought swiftly that this was the explanation she had been seeking. Why else should this
man, still a stranger, break his habitual silence?

But when Gerald added that although he was di-
vorced he would never marry again, she thought that
he was inviting her to be his mistress.

Yet, such an obvious and crude explanation did
not satisfy the continued enquiries of her mind, for
she sensed that he was in some way unusually moved
or perturbed.

But the casual words which would have stilled
the tension between them remained unspoken, for
she could not be indifferent to his attraction.

She was thrilled by his kisses, and his touch
awoke in her a flame-like response which was beyond her control.

Later she found herself crying, "No, no!" as he
held her in his arms.

Yet her protestations were as much to herself
as to him, for she knew that while he asked for her
surrender, he would not take her until she was ready.

Her own weakness, her truant body, frightened
and surprised her.

In the past she had found in men only the de-
lights of companionship, and she was afraid of this
desire which swept to one side, as logs in a swift-
flowing stream, all that she had thought was most
static in herself.

Away from Gerald she could view him dispas-
sionately, criticising character, ideas, and eccentricity.

Yet, in the instant of her uncertainty, the thought
of his lips and arms would send a tremor over her
whole body and a quivering flame would make her
ache and tremble.

Sitting in the moonlight, Pamela tried to expel
him from her mind, to merge herself into the calm
detachment of a world of impersonal beauty, into the
sea, cool and boundless.

Suddenly she wanted to feel the chill of deep

water, believing that in some way it could wash the fire of passion from her body and absolve her from desire.

Swiftly she slipped from her clothes, and, moving slowly, with a deliberation at once both proud and as selfless as a novice moving towards the altar to take her first vows, she walked into the sea.

The water crept slowly from ankle to knee, from knee to thigh, until finally the ripples broke silver and shining against the warmth of her breasts.

Then she swam a little, her breathing deepening as in the movement of her arms she knew a joy more buoyant than the sea which sustained her.

The water was very clear, but each stirring wave was magnified and reflected by the moonlight onto the smooth bottom of the bay, so that she swam in some strange, glamorous pattern, part of a mosaic of sea and sky.

She felt that she was submerged, caught back into the universe, which had given her being.

All her wonderings fell from her, so that for a moment she was supreme, God-like, and apart from everything save this merging through and beyond the confines of the flesh.

Dazzled, in a state of bliss, when finally she moved into shallow water again it was as though she had been baptised by water and then by spirit.

She was cold, but she had no thought for anything save her release from the chains and problems which had previously held her earth-bound.

With the water dripping from her body, she moved slowly from sea to shore, then raised her eyes to see by her clothes the dark silhouette of a man.

It was Gerald. Without hesitation she walked slowly towards him, for in this new birth of herself she knew no shame or false modesty; for the moment she was intact, absolute in mind and body, so that he could not disquiet or move her.

He did not speak as she picked up the white woollen coat she had worn over her thin dress, slipped her arms into the loose sleeves, wrapped it round her, and in silence sat down beside him.

When she was still, her feet deep in the warm sand, her arms enfolded across her breasts, feeling the wool of her coat against her nakedness, he asked:

"What power have you over me?"

But she did not answer or even turn her head towards him, and after a moment he continued:

"I think I hate you. At first I thought you were as other women, so I wanted you and meant to take you as I have taken others. But this evening after you left me I packed my clothes, ready to leave.

"I was going to go back to Paris, never to see you again, because you revived and resurrected something which I thought was dead, something which I would avoid as other men might try to cheat death.

"But when the taxi came I knew I could not go. I sent it away and then came here to fight against myself. Why can you do this to me? Why?"

There was an insistency in his voice, and such an expression of agony that Pamela was roused even from the glory which still held her apart; she had gazed upon Gerald and his world as from a cloud, seeing only a vague landscape which could neither stir nor invite her.

She looked at him now and her eyes were large and dark in the moonlit whiteness of her face.

She could think of nothing to say, could find no words within herself which might assist or stem this labour of rebirth.

After a long time he rose and went away into the shadows of the pines.

Slowly, as if she were descending to earth, Pamela felt the return of her own familiarity.

One by one the thoughts which had perplexed and worried her returned to their accustomed places, rippling smoothly but persistently in and out of her consciousness, so that the detachment she had felt was undermined, and gently, like a mist lifting over the sea, it vanished.

Then the significance of Gerald's coming, and of what he had said and the pain within his speech, came to her and lay before her judgement.

Once again she felt the tremor of desire, and in prayer she raised her face to the star-strewn sky, asking:

"What shall I do?"

But the heavens were silent, and she found no answer in the shadowed circle of the moon or in the silence of her heart.

'I am forsaken,' she thought, and she felt afraid until, gently, words and harmony began to form within her mind.

They separated themselves into a pattern, first one and then another, fitting together like pieces of a child's puzzle, until they were complete.

She recognised them, and saw him who had said them long ago, high in the little mountain City which was to be immortal by this love of which he spoke.

Were ours that gentle blossoming love which springs
From the broad bosom of our Mother Earth,
To join the heart of nature with the sky
For one brief moment,
And then play Creator.
'Twould be our sacrilege and shame to love.
But born too long to be forgotten,
Grown too deep to be denied,
This love is part of all we are, and may become.

So in the speech of the Abbot John, Pamela found an answer to her prayer.

She knew now what must be, and, against her decision which had crystallised and formed before heaven and her soul, there was no appeal.

She rose and dressed, and as she did so the last remnants of that ecstasy which had been hers fell away. She was depressed, sinking into an abyss of misery.

Pamela walked with dragging feet over the sand-dunes, in deep unhappiness now that there could be no future where she and Gerald were concerned.

In the garden of the Inn, Hans was sitting alone, pulling at his pipe, his violin beside him, shut for the night in its black case.

He made no sign, but Pamela knew that he saw her, and though at first she would have passed quickly in through the door and sought the privacy of her own room, she hesitated, turned, and went across the garden to him.

Without preamble or explanation she said:

"I must go away."

He took the pipe from his mouth.

"So," he said. "And where will you go?"

"I don't know," Pamela replied. "Help me. Where can I find quiet and peace?"

"If I could advise you of that," Hans said, "I should be offering you a talisman or the philosopher's stone for which wise men have searched all through the ages. There are quiet places in the roar of a city or in the midst of a desert, but peace for the individual can only be found within himself, and I have never attained it."

Pamela made a little gesture of despondency, as

one who would say that she has failed on every side; then Hans said:

"I too am going away. I am leaving tomorrow night for Tunis."

"You did not tell us. I had no idea," Pamela said in surprise, for they had dined together a few hours ago and there had been no mention of his departure.

"I had a letter this morning," he said, "but I was undecided and so I kept silent. There is a man I want to see, someone who will help me with my work in Germany; I had hoped that he could come here to me, but I find he has already left this country and gone to Africa.

"He is the link on which the success of my present missions turns or fails, and therefore I must put all thought of comfort aside and seek him. An hour ago I made enquiries, and I learnt that a cargo-boat sails from Quimper tomorrow on the night tide. The Captain will take a passenger."

"Oh, I am sorry," Pamela said impulsively. "I shall miss you."

"Yet you too must leave," Hans said. "Why not come with me?"

"Why not?" Pamela echoed. "Will you take me? But this is marvellous. I must go—I must, and thank goodness I have plenty of money."

"Oh, it will not be expensive," Hans replied. "It is only in small ships that I can afford to travel. It will be rough and none too comfortable. You don't mind?"

"Of course not," Pamela said eagerly. "Oh, Hans, you have solved all my problems for me. I am running away again, but I know it is the only thing I can do. But please, don't tell Gerald I am going."

"I will speak to no-one of your intentions," Hans said. "I will only do my part, and go to Quimper early in the morning to find out if it is possible for the Captain to take us both."

"Don't let him refuse!" Pamela said. "Please, Hans, be very firm and insistent. I don't mind how uncomfortable it is, so long as I can get away."

He nodded, and she knew that he would not fail her. On an impulse she put an arm round his neck and kissed his cheek.

"Good-night, dear Hans," she said. "I am so very, very grateful."

When she left him in the darkness, there was a smile on his lips as though he too was now content.

❋   ❋   ❋

Now that the moment of departure was upon her, Pamela thought of what little use she had made of her hours in Bugalé and that she should have learnt more of her brother.

But the days had drifted past and her contact with him had held no unusual depth of unity; she had but partaken of his company when he sought her out.

Now, in a kind of fear of losing more, in an effort which would grasp before it was too late a stream flowing away from her, Pamela rose and dressed.

As she descended the stairs she knew that her daydreaming had continued too long for her to encounter Ion at breakfast, for coming in from the garden she met Lisette and knew that already Ion had entered the hut for his morning's work.

So she drank her coffee alone, and, refusing the rolls and yellow butter which invited her, she crossed the road with determination and went towards Ion's sanctuary.

She did not hesitate when she opened the door, but she was relieved to find him sitting idle in the window, his hands unoccupied, and he smiled at her in welcome, as if glad that she interrupted his idleness.

Without further preamble Pamela told him of her plans to leave and that she was going because of Gerald.

"Last night," she said, "it seemed so clear, the only thing I could do, and yet this morning I am uncertain. Am I wrong, I am asking myself, not to stay when I believe that I have awakened within him that true love which he thought could never be his again? For I think it was that which made him afraid."

"And you?" Ion asked. "What do you feel towards him?"

"I too am afraid," Pamela answered, "not for him, but of myself. He has made me feel and know a part of me which up till now I was unaware existed, and yet it is not love, Ion. I know that, when I am honest. Not the love of which I have dreamed, of which I was certain I could, and might, know when I read your book."

She rose and stood beside him, her hands open in an appealing gesture, as if in her perplexity she threw aside all pretence and stood naked in search of truth.

"Is it a dream?" she asked. "Is such love, such freedom as I seek, just an ideal, never to be attained?"

Her words stirred Ion so that she knew he took her problem to himself, and struggled to answer it from the depths of all he knew, and from the heights of all he too had ever hoped for.

"Listen," he said. "I will tell you. I too once doubted, and yet found through my doubting a certainty which has never left me since."

Pamela sat down, curling her feet under her, lower than Ion so that she must raise her eyes to watch his face.

"I was in Paris," he said; "it was shortly after I had left you all in England. I had struggled, and I had come suddenly and quite unawares to the end of my resources, for while there was a possibility of selling anything I wrote, the power of creation had left me.

"The rent of the small attic where I lived was due, and I knew that the money must be found even while my mind was utterly barren. It was as though I had suddenly become a vacuum, a mere husk and shell, empty of all that power which at other times had seemed to me inexhaustible.

"For a day and a night I sat striving to force myself to recapture if only for a moment that which I had once known so well, and then a terrible fear came over me, and I rushed from my room down into the streets.

"It was night and the streets were dark, and deserted save for a prostitute who came towards me. But when she saw my face she thought I was ill and offered me money instead of herself, inviting me to eat with her. But I pushed her rudely aside, desiring no kindness, only to be alone with my despair.

"I walked until I came finally to the river as it moved swiftly under the many bridges which reflected themselves in its smooth surface. I climbed down from the quay until I stood at the water's edge, and there was the sound of its lapping and the swinging of many boats in its flow.

"I thought how I must die, and I saw myself taking the few steps which would bring me into the water. I felt how it would open for me, quickly soak into my clothes, and fill my shoes so that they would be heavy and a drag.

"I knew I must swim a few strokes so that I should find myself in the centre of the stream, and that then my will must paralyse my arms and legs, making them subservient to my desire.

"I felt how the water would close over my head; I would know the pressure, the weight of it, and the sensation of sinking.

"Then would come a moment of detachment when this choking mass of flesh was no longer mine, when I would find release and absolution for the body.

"I stood savouring what was to come, and in imagination I half-saw and half-felt my body sag away, carried as if it were a log upon the bosom of the tide.

"Then in that moment came a unity which transfigured and transformed me, merging the dark shadow of myself into the all which lay round. I became one with the water surging past, so that I was all and all was in me.

"I was the river and the lights reflected on its surface; I was the bridge which spanned it and the sky above. There was no division, but a unity which held each thing, everything, and myself.

"There were footsteps on the quay above; I was those footsteps. There were voices of the passers-by; I was those voices!

"How long I stood there, how long such identification lasted, I don't know, for all the barriers of time and space were lost.

"When finally I came upon myself again, I was like a man drunk and dazed with a happiness I cannot possibly describe. And all was changed—myself, the familiar roadways, the houses, and the sky.

"One man hurrying homewards in evening-dress gave me some money as he passed, and as I felt the coins touch my hand I laughed out loud, not in scorn but in joy that would not be repressed, and in surprise that money still existed in a new world which was my own.

"I gave the money to a woman whom I met, and passed on to the room I had left what seemed a century ago. I took up my pencil, lying where I had thrown it, and I wrote:

> *"I heard the beating of Death's wings,*
> *I sought with groping hands escape*
> *From all I knew without, within,*
> *Of life.*
>
> *I am that pulse of moving life;*
> *I am the river and its source;*
> *Life cannot end, nor death begin*
> *In me."*

After reading this to her, he said:

"When it was finished I realised that there were no words which could express or describe even to myself what I had found; but the desire for creation was with me again, and I knew that I must obey it. I began and finished a long story in French, and later it was published."

Ion paused. Then, as Pamela did not speak, he went on:

"And so must you remain true to your faith, accepting only what you believe."

"But you are speaking of faith, and I of love," Pamela said. "Are they the same?"

"To a man, not always; to a woman, invariably," Ion replied.

He laughed gently and added:

"What arguments such a statement would provoke

if I said it to anyone except you. And yet I believe it to be true, for women infuse their whole beings into the love they have for God or man, and it is impossible to divide in them where faith ends and love begins. While in men there can be and often is a deep severance."

"Do you think," Pamela said passionately, "that I shall ever find someone who will wish for, and be equal to, all that I can give?"

"Am I a prophet?" Ion asked. "And is there, as far as we human beings are concerned, any equality?"

Then he added:

"Go to Tunis with Hans. He will look after you. He is a great man and you can learn from him a much more rational outlook on life than Gerald or I can give you. Hans has tried by practical means to help the people he loves. Whether he has failed or succeeded, only the unwritten history of tomorrow can decide. He thinks he has failed. It will be good for him to have you."

"And you?" Pamela asked. "Are you going to stay here?"

Ion shrugged his shoulders.

"I don't know," he replied. "Sometimes I get a nostalgia for the mountains, at other times I am too lazy to pack my bags and be gone. Soon there will be snow in Switzerland, and then perhaps Lisette and I will go to a little chalet where we have stayed before, high up where the road ends and there is no-one save ourselves."

But he perceived that Pamela was not listening to him, and that there was a shadow on her half-averted face, as if her troubles still weighed heavily upon her.

So he was silent and he thought of how he had seen her, not yet fully come to her adolescence, but it was already heralded in her eyes by that faint bewilderment as child merges into woman.

It hurt him now that in the first travail of her heart he was excluded and must remain spectator, for in the decisions of love a woman is alone, so that when it comes to her like some communication from Heaven she is virgin in her solitude and can refuse or receive it only by herself.

Ion thought of how in her childhood Pamela had belonged in his mind to the moors and the river they both had loved, and now she was part with the sea and the pines, and he was amazed at the adaptability of women, in that for the men who love them they can become so completely merged in their surroundings.

He knew that she was at this moment an inseparable part of his hut, of the chair in which she was sitting, the desk her hands had touched, and the windows through which she gazed.

He wondered if on her journey to Tunis she would seem to Hans part of the ship and one with the roughness or the calm of the sea.

He knew that it was good for her to go, and that Gerald could not hold her even as her old life had been unable to.

He saw for the first time a plan of his own creation twisting through the lives of others.

The Forgotten City had come to Pamela as a revelation; to another it might be a slow tide creeping into consciousness.

To some it would be as a swift downpour; to others it would have the quality of sunlight.

And Ion was humbled in that he might fail to

translate the truth for others, yet elated because once he was assured he had succeeded.

*　　*　　*

"I will not creep away," Pamela said to herself, and she walked unwillingly yet determinedly down the road towards Gerald's studio.

It was afternoon, and already the hour at which he expected her had passed. She had planned at first to leave with Hans, and to let her absence and her departure explain itself.

But after the morning spent with Ion she had realised that she could not, in respect to herself, slink away. She must see Gerald, and tell him herself, so that he might not hear the truth from another.

She had stayed with Ion in his hut for hours, poring over the manuscript of his new book. And he offered her his thoughts to balance and transmit through the medium of her intuition to a deeper perfection.

She learnt from him that morning, for as always that which strikes a note of harmony within ourselves awakes the full octave, and thought floods upon thought, making an endless echoing music which continues long after the original note has been forgotten.

To Ion, Pamela was a source of inspiration; there was in her a simplicity of thought and expression which revealed all that was false and artificial in what was proffered to her.

Though more of Ion's book was destroyed than constructed during their morning's work, he knew that what they left was, without question, the best.

They had been late for the midday meal and found that Gerald had eaten and departed, leaving a message with Lisette that he was expecting Pamela later in the afternoon.

She had anticipated such a message, but the idea crystallised within her that she must go to him and not, as she had half-hoped more than determined, evade the issue.

Hans had not yet returned, but as she and Ion were drinking their coffee there was the noise of the autobus racing down the road, taking the corner into the village with that speed and total disregard of danger with which Frenchmen love to travel.

A few seconds later Hans came into sight, and as soon as she saw him Pamela knew that his mission had been successful and that they would embark that evening.

When they had talked for a while she rose and left them without explanation.

'If I do not go soon,' she thought, 'I may never go, or Gerald may come and look for me.'

She could not bear to meet him again before the gaze of the others, and as her hand touched the latch of his door she felt that her calmness was but a pretence, for her heart beat quickly.

She entered, and, as the windows were already shaded, she stood unseeing in the dim green light before she discovered that she was alone.

For a second she imagined that Gerald might have gone away, then the bark of a dog outside the tower told her that he was on the sands, and she saw him through the open doorway.

She moved quietly into the room, without calling him, and walked to where her picture stood on the easel.

He had been working on it during the night, and it was already half-finished. She looked; there was something wrong. The portrait lacked the strength and force which was characteristic of his work.

'It is the bitterness that is missing,' Pamela thought. 'The streak of hate which shows so plainly in his other work. This he has worked in love, and it is not good.'

And while she stood, afraid of what she sensed in the lines of her own pictured body and the half-averted head, Gerald entered.

He came carelessly, abruptly, into the studio, then stopped on seeing her and stood staring across the room at her with lowering brows and an expression which she did not understand.

She met his eyes bravely and said in a low voice:

"I am sorry this picture will not be finished. I am going away."

"When?" he asked.

"Tonight," she said; and when he did not speak again, she felt as if she had stabbed him unawares, and she added:

"I am sorry."

He came towards her, and she steeled herself; but she had misunderstood his action. He did not touch her, only stood beside her in front of the canvass.

"What do you think of your picture?" he asked.

Although she was surprised, she turned her face obediently towards the easel, seeking for words to express the truth without hurting him. While she hesitated, he spoke again.

"There is no need to answer me," he said roughly. "I know how bad it is. And because of what you see in the picture you have no need to be sorry for me. Like all women, you are imagining that at the touch of your hand and through your benevolent influence you can cast out devils.

"It sounds pretty enough, the legend of redemption through love, but it doesn't work like that in real life. You are right to go away, and when you have gone, don't torture yourself with the idea that you should have stayed.

"You cannot give me anything. All you can do is temporarily impair my work.

She would have spoken, but he went on:

"Oh, I know, I know, I know it all. Words can never make clearer what is already obvious. I think that I love you and you think so too, but I tell you that this is only desire translated, by being unsatisfied, into something which inflames not only my body but temporarily my mind.

"Don't imagine for one moment that you could alter me. Every woman is a missionary at heart; you are no exception. But I cannot live without my hatred of people and humanity!

"If you take that from me, there is nothing left, for I need it as a drug-addict needs drugs or a drunkard needs wine. It has grown to be part of me now, and without it I can no longer be myself or what I wish to be."

"But Gerald," Pamela said, "why do you let yourself be like this? Why?"

"You are surprised," Gerald answered. "Not at what I am but at what I have the honesty to say. That is what shocks you, the fact that a man may be what you call a sinner or a swine and admit to it."

She made a little sound but he continued:

"My answer is, because I like hating; even as a fakir enjoys the mortification of the flesh, as a masochist enjoys self-torture, so I revel in my bitterness. That is what I am, and I do not wish to be any different."

Seeing by her eyes that she did not believe him, but was thinking of last night in that moment when she, being betwixt sea and sky, had watched in detachment his love and want of her, he said:

"You are still deceived! Still imagining yourself the lady missionary! But don't you see that it is not you who has conjured up within me a ghost from a grave long forsaken."

He smiled at his own simile before he continued:

"No, it is not you, but a quality of yourself, a freshness as of something immaculate which is in you now. It is that which commands a response in me, passing for the moment beyond the desire of my body for yours.

"Yet look at it sanely, and see how soon, how quickly, such a thing can be dispelled. How long do you think you could retain that particular attraction once you surrendered yourself to me?"

He paused.

"And, having defiled you with my own mud, do you imagine you would mean more to me then than those others who have come into my life and passed from it again? There have been many women and none of them have meant more than an idea for a picture."

There were tears in Pamela's eyes, for Gerald's words stung and hurt her as though he had struck her.

She turned away from him, annoyed that he should see her distress, but as she turned he put his arms round her and drew her back.

He bent his head so that his cheek was against hers, and his voice, defiant, mocking, and cruel, changed as he said gently, and hardly above a whisper:

"Oh, my dear, I want you so."

But his words had bruised and numbed her so that the magic of his touch could not inflame her, and her indifference set her free.

"That is what I feared," she said almost angrily, "that we should part unhappily."

"And what did you expect?" he asked roughly, his tenderness gone. "Like all women, you want to end on what is called a 'happy note,' a nicely rounded chapter coming to a full stop, with no regrets and no untidy, tangled feelings left behind.

"Well, you have the satisfaction of knowing that all the readers of our story would say you were well rid of me. You have escaped inviolate, still a virgin, from a cad who would have contaminated you."

"Stop, Gerald! Will you not talk like that?" Pamela said. "If I loved you I would live with you and belong to you whatever you are. But I know that what I feel for you is not ..."

She stopped, for she found that there were no words to tell him how much she wished she could experience and capture the love in which she had set her faith.

Gerald laughed, but in his laugh there was no humour.

Only the disillusionment of one who for a brief moment has believed that he may evade the justice of life, and who finds in the eternal cause and effect no mercy and no reprieve, and so takes pride in his own defiance.

*   *   *

Back at the Inn, Pamela put her few belongings together; but her thoughts were with Gerald, and

while she knew that the half-hour they had spent together had made a gulf between them which now
could never be bridged, yet, woman-like, she blamed
herself.

For every contact of love, however small, is to a
woman a candle which is lit before the inner shine of
herself, and she would have it burn bright and eternal in the hearts of those who may have come within
her radiance.

As a visitor may enter some Church in a strange
town and, kneeling, offer a prayer and leave again,
remembering perhaps in after-years only the fra-
grance of the flowers before the altar, so may a man
yet retain when he is old a vision of the hand of a
woman he once loved, the echo of her voice, or perhaps the scent she used.

All else may have been forgotten—her name,
her eyes, her face—yet still that little flame of memory, burning bright, will keep in mind the pale reflection of the love long past.

But to love in pain, to know that all must vanish,
is to shame the woman for a failure of what must be
her life's true mission—to leave the life of every man
she meets in some particular lovelier because she
came.

Failure was hard upon Pamela as she moved
wearily from drawer to suitcase, for despondency,
like despair, makes even the physical limbs heavier,
as though the force of energy is dimmed and half-
quenched.

Nothing is more depressing than that which is inevitable in life, but she wished she could give herself
and many years of her life for the alteration of Gerald.

Now that the time was nearing for departure,
she felt that the journey to Tunis with Hans was

ridiculous and without purpose, and she asked herself:

"When I get to Tunis, what then?"

Below, Hans awaited her, his bags already packed, his precious violin beside him on the table; Lisette, talking to him as Pamela entered, looked up at her approach and smiled anxiously, for to women there is always adventure, and almost always some danger, in travelling.

The fear of it is ingrained by generations of men setting out in perilous ways before modern invention could keep them in touch with home.

Even today women fear voyages, for they are connected in their minds with leave-taking, and it is always women's fate to wave farewell.

The smallest journey will conjure in their minds the agony of good-bye, and they steel themselves to the shadow of a thousand deaths through the course of a lifetime.

"I am ready," Pamela said.

While she strove to speak lightly, there was in her expression something which made Hans ask:

"You are quite certain that you really wish to go?"

But Lisette, who saw and understood that this journey must be, saved Pamela from answering by her quick intervention, teasing Hans that now that the moment had come, he was afraid of his reputation and did not want the responsibility of being a chaperon.

He protested quite seriously, and Pamela knew that he was overjoyed not only that he should have a companion but that the companion should be herself.

As always when people are leaving, because the trivialities of everyday existence are somehow unim-

portant in comparison with the mileage they must
travel, silence fell.

However vast the distance in between, yet always there is that prelude of silent anticipation when
the commonplaces of conversation fall like a burden
from those who depart.

"I must come back here. I will come back here,"
Pamela vowed to herself as moving in the bus towards Quimper she had a last glimpse of the curved
coast and the green sea with the trees standing sen-
tinel beside it.

A sense of loss made her lean forward so as to
catch the last sight of Bugalé; in doing so, she saw
Lisette turn away before the bus was out of sight, to
take Ion's arm as if he was all that mattered and all
else an interruption.

They drove between the high hedgerows, stop-
ping every now and then to take up other passengers,
or to avoid animals which had strayed across the
road.

Hans did not speak; he sat, smoking his pipe, his
violin balanced carefully across his knees.

Finally the roofs of Quimper came into sight,
surmounted by the high tower of its Cathedral; then
he turned to Pamela and said in a voice of satisfaction:

"So we set out. It has begun already, our voyage
of discovery."

THE WISDOM OF THE YOGA APHORISMS OF PATANJALI

The more thou dost advance, the more thy feet pitfalls will meet. The path that leadeth on, is lighted by one fire—the light of daring, burning in the heart.

The more one dares, the more he shall obtain. The more he fears, the more that light shall pale.

No light that shines from Spirit can dispel the darkness of the nether Soul, unless all selfish thought has fled therefrom, and that the pilgrim saith:

"I have destroyed the cause: the shadows cast can, as effects, no longer be."

—*The Voice of Silence*

Chapter Seven

The ship creaked and groaned, but for the first time in three days the storm was less violent.

Pamela was neither afraid nor ill. She had been brought up by the sea and had spent too many days in fishing-boats.

But at the end of the first day Hans succumbed and she nursed him.

She despised herself for at first shrinking from the task, for she hated illness in all its forms, and while she fought against herself she was at the same time beset by great anxiety.

For Hans was too old to stand the strain and his heart seemed to be affected. He would gasp for air, and nothing she could do seemed to relieve him.

But at last they reached calm waters and Hans sat on deck in the sunshine, wrapped in rugs, while Pamela sat at his feet, looking at the calm of a blue sea which but reflected in greater depth the sky.

"It is just as I always imagined the Mediterranean to be," she said.

Then she smiled at her own enthusiasm, thinking how strange it was that one was always more pleased by what is familiar or expected than by something surprising or strange.

It is the home-making instinct within us, she

thought, which makes us seek familiarity in everything we encounter.

She had already likened the mountains of
Majorca, which they had left on their starboard side,
to the hills round Glenferry, and now quite unreasonably she was glad because her pictured vision of
the Mediterranean was fulfilled in its vivid blue and
calm of sea and sky.

Hans was white and haggard as if from a long
illness, and anxiously she wrapped the rug closer
round his legs, as though by ministering to him she
could drive health back into his body and dispel the
frailty which sat strangely as a disguise upon so large
a man.

It was hot, but a faint breeze filled the big sails
and kept them on their course without the assistance
of the engine.

'This is perfect,' Pamela thought; yet there was
a shadow over her happiness when she looked at
Hans.

It was not only his health, for now she thought
that he must have been nearer to death in the stress
and struggle of the storm than she had realised, and
in its shadows he had changed, as people often do
when they come near to that gateway into the unknown.

There was about him a detachment which was
completely alien. There had been an urgency about
him, and he gave, on acquaintance, the uncomfortable sense of someone who, more powerful than his
fellows, forces upon them vibrations from which they
instinctively recoil.

Now the Hans whom Pamela had known was
gone and a stranger had taken his place.

Deeper than weakness, and not to be explained

even by a lassitude which made his voice more gentle and less assertive, Hans was altered in himself.

But Pamela could not ask about or speak of this to him; she could only watch as one might behold the glory of the sun sinking low in the sky until, wrapped in the clouds, it no longer tells of activity but of rest.

Sitting on deck, they spoke for a time of little things, until Pamela said:

"Are you sad, Hans?"

He replied:

"Not if you mean sorrowful."

"What then?" she asked.

He did not answer for a long time, so that she thought he had not heard or did not wish to reply. Then, tired of waiting, just as her attention was about to be caught up in some fresh thought, he said:

"I wonder whether all men see clearly as they come towards the end of their journey how the things they thought to be the greatest are of infinitesimal size and value."

Pamela knew that he spoke not of the journey which must end in Tunis but of his life and his own voyage through it, and she answered:

"Can one judge? Is it not the old story of standing too close to the picture? Only later, much later in history and in the progression of a people, can one understand how great or small a part has been played by any individual."

But he would not be comforted or roused from some despair within himself, and he said:

"Waste is the cruellest thought of all, waste of energy, words, and the faith of those you have trusted."

'Soon he expects to die,' she thought, 'and this is his Gethsemane.'

She shrank from her imaginings and rushed to words to escape them.

"If you had your life over again," she said, "knowing no more than you knew when it started, would you alter much?"

When he had pondered, he answered honestly:

"No, for at the time everything I did seemed the most expedient thing to do, while now I realise how stupid I have been. I did not understand then that there was always an alternative."

And Pamela said:

"How, then, can you have any regrets? Surely they are only for people who, knowing what is best, and sensing what is right, yet choose another way."

She remembered how her father, many years ago, had explained in answer to her question the theory of rebirth.

She had been reading a book on the East and had found a reference to Karma and to reincarnation, which had puzzled her.

She had gone to him as she always did with her problems, and he had explained, taking books here and there from his well-stocked shelves, but relying not so much on the texts as on his own interpretation.

"It is like the third form, this world we know, which some call the third dimension," he said, "and in the third form, as at school, there are certain lessons which must be learnt and understood before the pupil can pass onwards to the fourth."

"You mean," Pamela said, "that one may come back many times to this particular world in different bodies."

"Exactly!" her father said. "Many terms, if you like."

"And in between?" Pamela asked. "I mean, when a man dies before he is reborn, what then?"

"Those are the holidays," her father said with a smile. "Only in a body can one learn, as long as one is attached to this dimension, and the accumulated knowledge gathered during one incarnation starts complete in the next."

"So that was why Mozart could play the violin at the age of four," Pamela said in a tone of triumph. "I have often wondered how that could be possible. Tell me more."

"It is only a theory," her father said. "I am not giving you a creed, and yet there is logic in it, and justice."

"And when finally we have learnt our lesson," Pamela went on, "when we are ready for the next form, what then?"

"If I could tell you that," her father said, "I should not be sitting here in the third dimension with you; but it is reasonable to suppose that what is possible for one man is possible for all—that is justice; that and only that can explain the world today, with high and low, rich and poor, suffering and pain.

"Those whom we believe were saints and Messiahs have shown us a height attainable by every individual and which, when he comes to it, will carry him forward into some new state of existence which here we can neither know nor contemplate."

"And Karma?" asked Pamela.

"Karma is the threads of your past life, running, growing, and accumulating now as they will in your future existences, until like a great river they can finally be traced from source to sea."

"I like the idea," Pamela had said.

She had been thrilled by what seemed to her a brilliant discovery, until she tried to explain it to her mother, from whom she received scant sympathy.

"A lot of ridiculous nonsense!" Mrs. Tarn had

said. "And your father has no right to go stuffing your head with his absurd Eastern theories. The Bible is good enough for me, and if you want to know your future life, read what is written in it, and you won't find anything there about such rubbish."

Almost resentfully Pamela obeyed her, wanting with an obstinacy which had its roots in her Scottish blood to find some argument to refute her mother and prove her wrong.

She thought that she was defeated, until illuminatively she came upon the text in which Christ, speaking to His disciples, asks:

"Whom say the people that I am?" And they said: "John the Baptist, but some say Elias, and others say that one of the old prophets is risen again."

Jesus had accepted without surprise the belief in rebirth.

What else could be meant? she asked herself. But when she had read and pondered on this passage, she felt no desire to confront her mother with what she had found; instead, she accepted this new addition to her own faith secretly and without further discussion.

*   *   *

It was in the early morning that the *St. Anna* came up the wide basin of sea-flooded land and so to the harbour of Tunis.

Pamela, standing alone, watching the grey water break to the prow of the boat, felt an expectancy and a tremor within her beyond the reason that the journey was at an end.

It was as though all that had happened in the past weeks had been planned for this moment when she should set her foot on a strange shore and encounter for the first time a country which, because it was part of the East, was shrouded in glamour.

"It is because of Hans that I feel the importance of the journey," she said to herself. "For without me he might have died, and because my presence was necessary to him, I am confused with a feeling of fatality."

But she knew that her explanation sprang not from instinct but from reason, and she turned again to that expectation which possessed her as she looked towards the flat roofs and the white buildings of Tunis.

Soon the moment came for them to say good-bye, and Hans was still so weak that the men helped him climb the narrow companionway to the deck and guided him over the gang-plank.

The Captain and the crew were touched by the little present of money he gave them, and would have refused it had he not insisted.

Pamela shook them by the hand and they smiled at her their goodwill, and wished her God-speed.

They were simple men, and she had grown to know them well, so that it was as though she left behind not only their friendliness but also all their families, their interests, and their ambitions, for they had talked to her of all that they knew and loved.

When they were finally ashore she turned back two or three times to wave her hand in farewell, and always they replied with raised caps, until finally she was out of sight.

Then the crew of the *St. Anna* settled to the serious task of unloading their cargo.

When they had climbed a little way, slowly because of Hans's frailty, they took a taxi.

The sun shone boldly on the flat-roofed white houses and cast strange shadows from the palm trees which waved their large leaves languidly in the sea breeze.

There was the darkness of deep archways, and the shuttered of deep-set windows gave the whole city an air of mystery. A half-glimpsed courtyard, the women covered from head to foot in black garments, the men staring with bold eyes and flicking fly-whisks as they smoked or drank outside the houses—these things filled Pamela with delight.

The taxi stopped at tall iron gates which opened onto another door, deep-set in a stone wall; here was the Hotel where they were expected, and of which Hans had already spoken to Pamela.

It was a famous Inn, yet the tourists would never have heard of it, and the travellers who journeyed for amusement would pass it by, not knowing that here was what they often sought but failed to find.

But to men who travelled with a purpose, and to those people whose reputation depends not on society but on their discrimination in serious matters, the House of the Star in Tunis was what they needed.

The Inn-keeper was a tall man with Arab and Jewish blood intermingled in him, and Pamela thought that if one studied his face for a century one would learn no more of what lay hidden in his mind and feelings.

He made them welcome, and when Hans had found that the man he sought had not yet arrived, they were shown to their bed-rooms.

From the outside, the House of the Star had seemed a very small place, for there was but the doorway and the low white building without windows blindly facing the road.

Yet within it was a labyrinth of passages and of rooms looking onto small courtyards where fountains played and palm trees sheltered small beds of brilliant flowers from destruction by the sun's strength.

Pamela sat in her window, listening to the tinkle of the water falling into the stone basin above which it sprayed.

Hans's room was next to hers, and, entering when he answered her knock, she found him sitting in a chair, his clothes unpacked.

He looked ill, and she was afraid and sent a servant for brandy.

* * *

Pamela's deepest impression of Tunis was one of brilliant sunshine as a contrast to shade so deep and so impenetrable that she could absorb only the superficial beauty it offered her.

Even in imagination she could not sense what was hinted at but never revealed.

Yet the little that was shown to a foreigner did not escape her, and she felt a kind of joy as people do when they come suddenly upon new customs and new conditions which invigorate the beholder by their very strangeness.

Even as the dances of African natives and their weird music can wake a response in the most staid and conventional onlooker, so Pamela, moving through the narrow, twisting passages of the native bazaar, identified herself with the East.

The heat of the sunlight on her body and the warm, heavy air which carried on it some breath of the sun-baked desert thrilled her; she was a stranger, yet she absorbed some substance of all that was round her.

Hans was not well enough to move from the Hotel; besides, he was expecting his friend to come to him that afternoon, and so Pamela walked with a guide.

Unmistakably European in her white linen dress

and broad-brimmed hat, she attracted immediate attention.

But she was saved from the attentions of the beggars and the curiosity of the children by the care and peremptory commands of her attendant.

He piloted her from shop to shop, in many of which she could watch the native craftsmen twisting bars of silver into jewelry of strange shapes and designs and setting in it semi-precious stones of curious colours.

There was a street of locksmiths, another of leather-workers, and one of embroiderers.

Weavers wove stories into their carpets, and their wares would travel all over the world bearing the imprint not only of their maker but of his dreams.

Dark eyes, heavily outlined in mascara, stared at Pamela from above the close veils of a yashmak, and beggars with revolting sores and mutilated limbs cried out to her for alms.

Children, goats, tourists, and Arabs thronged through the tiny streets, and often Pamela would encounter a pungent smell where the street-vendors offered strange and unwholesome-looking cakes and sweetmeats kept hot on small carts fitted with braziers.

At every tiny shop in which wares had been displayed for her approval she had been offered tea made of many diverse and strange leaves, and in courtesy to her host she sipped from the tiny cups which were brought by salaaming servants.

"I never want to taste tea of any sort again," she told Hans when she arrived back at the House of the Star and found him waiting for her in the cool of the courtyard.

Then the words with which she would have told him of her afternoon's sightseeing were checked,

for she saw that he was drawn and pale, with the air
of a man who has received a shock.

"How are you?" she asked, and then added:
"Didn't your friend come to see you?"

Hans shook his head.

"No," he said in a low voice. "He could not keep
the appointment, but he has sent me a letter."

And Pamela knew that the letter must have contained bad news, for otherwise Hans would not look
so old and grey. 'A man without hope,' she thought
to herself.

After a while Hans spoke of other things, but she
felt that his attention wandered away from her and
that he was hurt beyond expression.

There is nothing worse, Pamela thought, than
being disappointed, not only in what we had anticipated but in a friend whom we trust.

Later, they dined, sitting downstairs in a small
place set apart for them, for there was no main din-
ing-saloon, the visitors of the House of the Star pre-
ferring to be served in private or to seek their meals
elsewhere.

Pamela talked and tried to interest Hans in
what she was saying, but he made no pretence of eating, and soon she too felt her appetite failing.

Their dinner finished, he rose heavily to his feet,
and he had to be half-carried up the narrow wooden
stairs to his room.

Pamela sat and talked to him for a while, and
then, after a time, as though he could not keep his
mind off what was troubling him, he picked up some
of the papers which lay on the writing-table and
started to speak of them.

"This is the result of over four months' hard
work," he said. "I had hoped that I could find some

way of getting them printed and distributed in Germany, but it is not to be."

His voice was not bitter but tired, as though he accepted failure and was not prepared to challenge it.

"But there must be other people who can help you," Pamela said. "Don't be despondent, Hans."

But he shook his head.

"A year ago I would have forced someone to help me," he replied. "I would have stormed against opposition, and in my very determination I would have vanquished it. Now I cannot."

"But why?" Pamela asked, even while she knew the answer.

"I am tired," Hans answered. "Tired of an unending struggle which has eventually defeated me. All my life I have fought, all my life has been given up to one cause or another which I believed to be essential for the well-being of the people, and now I wonder if it was worthwhile."

"But, Hans," Pamela protested, "we have talked of this before. You know what wonderful things you have done, what a help you have been to thousands of people."

"I wonder," Hans replied. "I have incited them to revolt and half-heartedly they have obeyed me, but I wonder now if I was not only anticipating the natural course of events which in time would have altered and improved without rebellion and without the martyrdom of those who rebelled.

"Men have been shot," he went on, "men have died, because I made them fight. I feel now as if I had no right to drive any human being to his death."

"But that is morbid," Pamela said. "You are ill, and these things are worrying you while you are not strong enough to see what is true and what is false."

She spoke earnestly, and something in her face, turned towards him, and the eagerness with which she would comfort and help him, moved Hans, so that he put a hand upon her shoulder and smiled at her.

"You are a great comforter," he said, "and a wonderful companion. You have shown me, my dear, how much I have missed all these long years alone."

"There are many more years in which you can make up for it," she said, but her words sounded overly hopeful even to herself.

A sudden fear for him made her, as she said good-night, bend down and kiss him on the cheek.

After she had left him she stood for a long time in her room, listening, although why she did not know.

She told herself that she was listening for the very faint music of his violin, for he had asked her to place it in its case beside him. But her ears strained for something else, for a reassurance, but in what way she could receive it she did not know.

It was with a sense of relief that finally she heard the first sweet notes of music come gently through the partition of their rooms.

He played very softly, for Hans was afraid of disturbing other guests in the Hotel. Yet, when he desired his music it was for him an insatiable craving, as a man might long desperately to touch and fondle the woman he loves.

'All is well,' Pamela thought, and with a smile she started to undress.

Suddenly there was a rasping note, a discord, as though the bow had slipped on the strings ... and then silence.

For a moment Pamela hesitated; then, swift with fear, she ran from her room and knocked at the adjacent door.

There was no answer, and after a second she turned the handle and entered. Hans had fallen across the foot of his bed; in one hand he held the bow, and from the other his beloved violin had slipped to the floor.

'He is dead,' she thought.

With a cry she hurried forward and strove to raise him. But he was too heavy, and wildly she ran into the half-darkened passage.

Some few doors away she saw a man walking away from her.

"Please!" she called, and as he turned, for a moment it seemed to her that he was someone she knew, someone familiar.

"Help me!" she cried. "Get a doctor."

He came nearer and she realised that she had been mistaken, that he was a stranger.

"Is someone hurt?" he asked. "Can I be of assistance?"

He followed her, without further words, through the open bed-room door.

He touched Hans's forehead, and then together they managed to lift him onto the bed.

His mouth and eyes were open, and the expression on his face was as though he had experienced sudden pain. The stranger loosened his shirt and felt for his heart.

Then, as though he saw that there was nothing to be done, he said:

"We must have a doctor."

"Is he dead?" Pamela asked.

There was no hysteria in her voice; she was calm, for she already knew the truth, and faced it with fortitude.

"I am afraid so."

His answer brought no tears to her eyes, but a sudden gasping breath escaped her as if she were suddenly immersed in deep water.

After a moment she bent and picked up the violin and placed it beside Hans.

"You will wait here?" the stranger asked.

When she nodded, he said:

"I will send a boy and come back."

Closing the door gently behind him, he left Pamela alone.

She sat at the foot of the bed and stared at Hans. So this was death, this sudden cessation of movement, the separation, in an instant, of body and life.

"Was there anything else?" she asked herself. "If so, what?"

Was the Hans she had known lying here, or had he gone, leaving behind only the shell which had housed his body?

"I ought to pray," she thought, and yet she could not, for her feelings were numbed by shock.

Only her brain seemed at work, independent of her will, questioning, criticising, and outside of herself, as if her mind were a spectator, separate from herself and all her emotions.

She was not afraid, but in the silence she found herself listening, half-thinking that Hans breathed, and that the stranger had been mistaken.

What if it was all a dream and they would both awake?

It was but a few minutes before she heard footsteps outside, and yet in that time she stood in a no-man's land in which death was so near that it was hard to believe that she herself could not also creep away from her body.

The shadows on the walls, the bedspread which

had slipped to the floor, the crumbled and torn mosquito-net, the grey of Hans's hair against the white pillow, these things she saw with her eyes.

Yet her inner being was caught up in a desire to feel, to know, and to reach him wherever he might be.

When finally the man who had helped her entered the room, followed by the keeper of the Inn, he exclaimed at her white face and haggard-looking eyes.

"You look ill," he said gently, as one might speak to a startled child. "Sit down."

He brought her a chair, and then he spoke to the Inn-keeper in Arabic. Pamela heard Hans's name pass between them.

"Hans Schaeffer?" the stranger exclaimed in surprise, and he looked intently at the dead man.

"Is he some relation of yours?" he asked Pamela.

"No," she said, with an effort, and her voice was hoarse, seeming to come from a great distance.

"In that case," he went on. "I think we can spare you much trouble with the police and the authorities. That is, if you would like me to do so."

"Thank you," she said simply. "There is only one thing I would like done."

"What is that?" he asked.

"Will you see that his violin is buried with him?"

The stranger nodded and the Inn-keeper assured her that it would be done.

"Why don't you go to your own room?" the stranger suggested. "I will see to all that is necessary, and I will come to you later, after the doctor has gone."

"Thank you," Pamela said, and rose obediently, as if she were a child.

She did not understand that they would move

the body and that this was her last sight of Hans. Going quietly between the two men, she went out through the door and closed it behind her.

Alone in her bed-room, she fell on her knees, not beside the bed but at the window, and felt the soft, still, warm night air upon her cheek.

She saw the sky above the flat roofs, and in it shone great stars, not hanging as though they were jewels, but as points of light fiercely piercing their way to earth. Then, without storm, so gently that their coming was almost imperceptible, her tears came.

"Hans is dead," she told herself, but the words seemed false and unreal.

His body was still in the next room; Hans, the man who she had nursed through a storm at sea, the companion whom she had grown to love with a deep tenderness.

"Hans is dead," she whispered, and the words came from her lips with a little hissing sound, so that she was startled by her own utterance.

Yet she felt no tragedy of spent emotion, but a loss as if she stood on an empty platform from which a train had departed bearing someone she loved. Hans had gone.

He was not in the room beyond, nor in that dim mist which had oppressed her but a few moments ago. He was gone, but she remained and there could be no severance of that which had united them in affection.

That would continue within herself and was therefore alive.

All that had made her a help and a comfort to him in his last hours, all the hours they had spent in each other's company, made an unbreakable chain until they met again.

There could be no disintegration of love.

Pamela raised her eyes to the sky and knowledge was hers beyond expression, beyond words and conscious thought, yet more real to her than the floor beneath her knees and the iron balustrade on which her fingers rested.

Truth came to her as easily as her tears, flowing into her consciousness with that unheralded arrival as a breeze can enfold a tree, to raise poignantly each leaf before one can say, "This is a beginning of it."

While still she knelt she heard the sound of voices and the tramp of heavy feet, but she remained at her window until after a long silence there came a knock at her door.

THE WISDOM OF THE UPANISHADS

That which is perfect is a Being, who hath comprehended and included all things in Himself and His own Substance, and without whom, and beside whom, there is no true Substance. For He is the Substance of all things, and is in Himself unchangeable and immovable, and changeth and moveth all things else.

For when the vain imagination and ignorance are turned into an understanding and knowledge of the truth, the claiming anything for our own will cease of itself. Then the man says:

"Behold! I, poor fool that I was, imagined it was I, but behold! it is, and was, of a truth, God!"

—*Theologia Germanica*

when it comes to her like some common things from Heaven she is virgin in her solitude to receive it only by herself.

She thought of how, in her childhood Pavel had burned in his mind to the remotest time they must had loved, and now she was next, right to

Chapter Eight

'This is how I shall always remember Tunis,' Pamela thought.

She was sitting under the shelter of a striped awning, and her view was of the busy street with its cars, trams, and flower-sellers, similar to thousands of other main thoroughfares all over the world.

On the table beside her stood a champagne cocktail, and she had wondered at Bruce Carrington's choice when he had ordered it.

There was something unsuitable in the golden wine in the long glasses. 'Drinks symbolise occasions,' she thought. 'Champagne for gaiety, beer for monotony, port for conversation, cocktails for triviality.'

This was the time for none of these drinks, for they had just come back into the town from the little Christian cemetery where Hans had been laid to rest.

Bruce Carrington had not asked Pamela's permission but had stopped the carriage at the fashionable Hotel which looked over the main street, and, having invited her to seat herself in the courtyard, he called a waiter and ordered drinks.

She was content not to question him; for, from the moment she had asked his help in the darkness of the passage, he had taken things into his own hands, saving her from all troubles and enquiries which inevitably attend sudden death, and especially that of a stranger in a strange land.

Now that he could do no more for Hans, it appeared that he must turn his attention to her.

He must have been aware that she was not faint but dazed when they drove away from the cemetery. She felt as if she were but a shadow without substance or stability, but the drink he had ordered for her was reviving.

Tumultuously, reality forced its way back, she became alive again, her numbed senses were released, and her surroundings became as clear-cut as a silhouette.

There was a caged bird singing in one of the windows above them, and Pamela heard its clear notes above the noise of motor-cars and the jingle of traffic.

A small, shaggy dog came in from the street and went from table to table seeking scraps.

'I shall remember both the bird and the dog,' Pamela thought, and then wondered at herself.

There was a boy across the street, holding under his bare arm a large bundle of newspapers. He called in a shrill voice to the passers-by, and men stopped to buy.

"Already Hans's death will be cried in London and in Berlin," she said to herself. "Every newspaper will speak of him and of his strange and varied career."

But none could describe the man she had known, the man who had shown her a side of his nature which his critics would not have believed existed—gentle, at times tender, desolate, and humble—strange adjectives with which to describe one of the greatest agitators of the century.

Now she felt that she must speak of him, and she could do so without sorrow and without tears, because she knew no unhappiness for him personally; only a regret that she could see him no more.

He had come to the end of what he could give; already he had begun to doubt his own faith, to regret the past rather than plan the future.

It was better that he should leave the world, to which he had given years of service, before in final bitterness he questioned not only himself but the sincerity which had driven him onwards.

Speaking quietly, as if she talked more to herself than to her companion, Pamela told of those moments after Hans's death when she had stood alone in his room.

She had felt not the freedom of an imprisoned spirit but the repression of her own imagination, which could not find him.

"I have seen many people die," Bruce Carrington said, "and it has always seemed to me that when a man is prepared and ready for death, the moment comes to him with a relief which is almost a joy.

"It is as though he stands outside a house, having asked admittance—then his waiting is at an end and the door is opened to him. In such men I have seen not surprise or even amazement on their faces at the first moment of release, but a contentment as if they came again to something familiar and beloved.

"Only those who are surprised by death, who have no time for thought or preparation, leave behind them an atmosphere of resentment and regret."

Pamela thought of her father's death, his calmness, and the final moment when she had known that he was once again at Glenferry.

This man, Bruce Carrington, was right.

'He understands,' she thought, 'what I say and mean more clearly than anyone else I have ever met before.'

And she looked at him with critical eyes, striving to find in what particular he differed from other men she had known.

He was tall, and there was about him a quiet as one might find in a deep pool of still water.

He was neither dark nor fair and his features were not particularly noticeable, being clear-cut, with the small bones and square jaw characteristic of many Englishmen.

His shoulders were broad and his head set well upon his body, as with men who have spent the greater part of their lives on horseback. His hands were thin, his fingers sensitive; like his face, they were tanned a deep brown by the sun, and he had the air of one who has lived in the East.

There was a suggestion of perception of one who must often have been in danger and thus grown alert to the slightest sound.

There was nothing peculiar about him, nothing that one would describe as characteristic in voice or bearing, and yet there was nothing commonplace about him.

'He is a man who has done things in his life,' Pamela thought, and then could not explain to herself how or why she should think so.

Already they had spent hours together, and while Pamela had told him much of herself she was still in ignorance of him.

A great deal of what she told him had been not in confidence but of necessity, for journalists representing newspapers all over the world had been telephoning the House of the Star for details of Hans's death.

Bruce Carrington had contrived that no mention of Pamela appeared in any paper.

Only the proprietor of the Inn and himself were aware that she had accompanied the dead man on his visit, and there was no mystery woman to intrigue and startle suburban homes into speculation.

"I do not know why you should do this for me," Pamela had said again and again. "I cannot tell you how grateful I am."

He had replied conventionally enough that he must help his countrywoman, and that it was easier for him to arrange things than that she should seek protection at the British Consulate.

She told him of the storm at sea, and he had exclaimed at the stupidity of an old man travelling in such a fashion when his heart was so bad.

"He might have died at any moment," he told her.

Cables and telephone messages kept arriving every few moments, demanding more details.

"I had no idea he was such a famous person," she said.

She tried, sitting at the marble-topped table, to tell the man facing her of Hans's kindness, his love of music, and his affection for her brother.

As she had requested, his violin had been buried with him, and she thought he would be glad to know that his "well-beloved" would never fall into careless hands.

"I saw Hans Schaeffer once many years ago in Homburg," Bruce Carrington said.

"Did you meet?" Pamela asked. "Or hear him speak?"

"I heard him speak," he answered, "and it was an occasion I shall never forget. He had changed considerably, and that is why I did not recognise him at first and was surprised when I heard his name."

"Tell me about his speech," Pamela said.

"It was shortly after the war, when there was much internal trouble in Germany. The people were starving, and starving men have much to gain and little to lose by violence. Some of them had raided a baker's shop, and during the struggle which ensued the baker had been killed and two of his assistants badly injured.

"The men were caught by the police and three of them were sent to penal servitude, but the ring-leaders—both under twenty-five years of age—were condemned to death.

"It was a savage sentence, but the authorities were afraid that the populace was getting out of hand, and thought that by making an example of one case they would have less trouble in the future.

"Your friend Hans started a petition to save the lives of the sentenced men. He spoke the day before their execution in the market-place at Homburg, and I happened to be passing through the city at the time.

"He was tremendous, an amazing orator, with a flow of language in itself unusual, apart from the fact that it was combined with a sincerity which made every word balanced and powerful as a bullet.

"The people listened to him in absolute silence. He started to speak quietly and gradually worked towards a dramatic and almost frenzied climax.

"I do not believe for one moment that there was any artifice in what he did; it was entirely natural and spontaneous.

"He inspired not only his audience but himself with his words until he was galvanised by a force that was almost frightening to watch.

"It is difficult to look unmoved on a man torn by his own passionate emotions. I felt that at any moment his last vestige of control would go. He was in-human, and terrifying in some ways. If he had fallen down in a fit I should not have been surprised.

"The whole crowd were affected by him as I was. They were tense, hardly breathing as they lis-tened, for fear that they should miss one word of what he said.

"Then just when I believed it was impossible for humanity to stand such a strain, the police arrived. The crowd looked like it was becoming very rough, and I slipped away."

"But what happened?" Pamela asked. "Did he save the men?"

"I don't know," he answered. "That is an unin-teresting climax to my story, but I never knew the end of the case in question because I left Germany that night, and such a familiar occurence for that country as the execution of two men was not likely to be reported in the foreign Press."

"Oh, I wish I knew," Pamela said. "I would like to think Hans had saved them."

"No-one could have tried harder," her companion said consolingly.

There was a pause while both sipped their drinks, then he asked, "What are your plans for the future?"

There was sunlight on the marble courtyard and a long finger of it, evading the shadows, touched the edge of Pamela's white dress.

The bird somewhere above them still sang, and she heard the music of tiny bells which hung on the harness of the horses.

She could not force her mind away from what was round her, from the consciousness of tangible things, from the sun and shade, from the face of the man to whom she spoke.

Almost stupidly she echoed his words:

"My plans?"

"You cannot stay alone in Tunis," he said gently.

Pamela thought of the many miles which divided her from England, and of the far greater distance which separated her in mind from her mother and the life she had lived in London for years.

It was only a few weeks since she had come away, driven, by the story of a legend, into the lives of new people and strange events.

'I went to find Ion,' she thought, 'and instead I found Gerald and Hans.'

They had not meant more to her than her brother, but they had forced themselves upon the surface of her attentions so that she must be more concerned with them.

They had carried her into their own lives so that the way she had sought to Ion, and to him alone, had been forgotten and laid aside.

Now at the question of her future she knew she could not return to Bugalé. She had left it because of Gerald, and he might still be there.

She could not be an outsider, almost an interloper, in the lives of Ion and Lisette. They did not need her; they were complete, their love making them utterly self-sufficient.

'Where can I go?' she wondered silently. 'What can I do?'

At the thought of Cowton she shrank even while she knew that her affection for Arthur was strong and his love for her unchanging.

To return home seemed to her now to be a betrayal of her promises to herself, of all that she had hoped for and believed in when she had taken the boat to France.

She had sought to resurrect within herself the

memory of what had been and what was still there, if she could find the way to attainment.

"I have no plans," she heard herself saying, "and nowhere to go."

"But that is absurd," Bruce Carrington answered. "I cannot leave you here. Will you let me cable to your brother—you have spoken of him—or to your family?"

Pamela shook her head, then she asked:

"Must I decide this moment? Let me think."

She almost pleaded with him, so that as if lightly he disclaimed responsibility.

"But of course," he replied.

They finished their drinks, and when he had paid, Bruce Carrington rose.

"Shall we be moving on?" he asked, and Pamela picked up her sunshade and bag.

Again she had the impression that this place where they had stopped and rested was vivid and of importance not only now but forever.

Bruce was waiting for her, his face towards her, his head uncovered for a moment in the sun, and once again she had that queer sense of familiarity about him as though they had met before.

But she could not as yet remember where or when.

*   *   *

Bruce had not asked Pamela to dine with him, but as she descended the stairs, ready for a lonely meal, he had come through the outer door and after a moment's hesitation had suggested that they should eat together.

She had accepted joyfully, for she had the feminine complex not only of disliking her own company but also of losing all appetite if she had no-one to eat with her.

Another place was laid for Bruce in the small room with its gilt mirrors and pale hangings, and he ordered a bottle of light wine, which was brought to them surrounded by ice.

At first they had talked of trivial things—the heat, the strangeness of the Hotel itself—but the conversation must eventually be of Hans, as the thought of him was uppermost in their minds.

"I have just received a cable from Paris," Bruce said, "asking if he left any unpublished manuscripts."

"There are several," Pamela answered. "They are in my room at the moment."

"I had all his personal papers sent in to you," Bruce replied. "I thought perhaps you would sort them out. Do you know if he has any relations who will claim them?"

"I think not," Pamela answered.

"Then it would be best for you to decide what shall be kept and what destroyed."

"He had recently finished several articles. I have not read them, but I will look through them tonight and give you those which are complete in the morning."

"You think that he would want his work published posthumously?" Bruce asked.

"But why not?" Pamela replied. "Surely what he attacked or supported but a few days ago cannot be altered by his death. He was not a mere figurehead."

"Perhaps you are right," Bruce said doubtfully, "but I cannot help feeling that Schaeffer, in the last few years, had become a practicably negligible influence. Interest in his work now is only because for the moment he is news."

"I see what you mean," Pamela answered, "and yet I would like if possible for Hans to give his last words to the world; but it will be easier for me to judge when I have read the manuscripts."

An ice was replaced by dessert plates, and a large basket of fresh fruit was brought to the table.

"When do you leave here?" Pamela asked.

"I do not know," Bruce replied. "Any day now. I am awaiting instructions."

"What do you do?" Pamela asked.

Then, feeling that perhaps such a question was impertinent, she added:

"I am sorry if that sounds curious. I only wondered when you used the word 'instructions.' "

"It sounds rather formidable, doesn't it," Bruce said with a smile. "I expect you are imagining me in the Secret Service or some dangerous diplomatic mission."

Pamela laughed.

"Of course that is what you ought to be," she said. "It would make a perfect story. Instead, I expect you travel in hardware or are here on some dull business connected with currency."

"For many people that is anything but dull," Bruce said drily. "I had a friend who spent his whole life studying foreign exchange. He made little money, for that was not the reason he did it. He found that it was to him a series of endless thrills."

Pamela knew that for some reason Bruce did not intend to answer her original question, and because of his reticence, what had been but a passing curiosity became a strong desire to know more of him.

Never before in her life had she met anyone who gave her that sense of ease which was never disturbed even when silence fell between them.

There was, she thought, a companionship about him which gave her not only security but another feeling, which she recognised as happiness.

She wanted to talk with him, and the subject was immaterial. She wanted to hear him answer her, to listen to his voice, though she dared not as yet ask herself the reason why.

As if to lead her away from the memory of her unanswered question, Bruce began to speak of Scotland; already he knew it was the one place on earth she really loved.

"When I am old," he said, "I have promised myself a small lodge on the west coast. It is a dream, but I would like to pass my last years in sight of the hills of Skye."

In delight that they should both love the same things, Pamela talked of her girlhood, surprised at her own powers of expression and description.

"Once I was engaged to a Scottish girl," Bruce said, and as he spoke something seemed to stand still in Pamela's heart. "It was in the last years of the war. I was very young, not quite eighteen, and we spent my leave sailing in the Western Isles."

"And you didn't marry her?" Pamela asked.

She was surprised by the urgency of her question and her eagerness for his answer.

"No," he said. "It was a youthful romance, started and ended in the fever of war. When I came home Muriel found me very humdrum without my uniform, and I found her a very pretty girl but with nothing that I wished for in a wife."

"And what do you want in a wife?" Pamela asked.

His answer seemed to hold an importance out of all proportion to a casual conversation made across a dinner-table.

She watched his hand as he raised the tiny green coffee-cup to his lips. She heard the faint tick of a clock at the far end of the room, and saw the shadow of him thrown by the light on the table against the white wall.

'It is a big shadow,' she thought, 'and he is not a big man.'

She could taste the wine in her glass, move her hands as she cut with a silver knife the fruit which lay on her plate, yet everything waited for the answer to her question.

'Answer!' every nerve in her body urged him. 'Answer,' she said with her eyes, as she raised them to his face and saw that he was not looking at her but staring ahead.

There was determination and strength in his expression and a suggestion of something else, something she did not understand.

She tried to speak lightly, but her voice was low and the words came strangely even to herself, for when she could bear it no longer, when she must know, she said:

"You haven't answered me."

"Haven't I?" he said quickly, as if she recaptured his attention, which had wandered a great distance away. "Well then, I will tell you. I shall never marry."

As he spoke, Pamela knew unmistakably that she loved him.

'This is unreal,' she thought to herself; 'it can't be true that here, without preliminary and without reason, I should discover that I love this man, of whom I know nothing.'

Yet the knowledge would not be denied. It flooded over her whole being in a glory that would not be dimmed even though, because of what he had said, she was afraid.

'Why?' she asked herself silently. 'Why?'

She remembered that first moment when she

had seen him in the darkness of the passage, how there had been something familiar which had made her half-recognise him.

She knew now that Bruce was not a stranger but someone towards whom she had travelled inevitably since that moment when she had risen from her bed at Cowton because of an inner command.

Love enfolded and enveloped her, for there is no moment when love begins; it is there or it is not. One is conscious of the full force and strength of it; there is no preliminary whisper.

Pamela knew now that a few hours ago, when they had sat in the courtyard, she had loved Bruce then with the whole depth of her being.

The bird which had sung, the dog which had moved from table to table, the noise of the traffic, and the murmur of voices had all been part of that love.

By putting out her hand she could touch his.

'But,' she thought, 'would that bring him closer to me?'

What did he feel for her? she wondered, and she could not believe that he could resist this power which had brought them together.

To him also would come, if it was not already in him, this love which, though a miracle, was yet inevitable.

Pamela felt herself trembling, so that when he held a lighted match for her cigarette it was with difficulty that she held it steady for him.

The blue smoke between them was, as the conversation, something which kept Pamela from crying out her love.

She dared not, and yet something impatient within urged her to dispense with all that was unnecessary, to make haste because time was passing.

'Time does not matter,' she thought. 'It has always been here, this love, and it will always remain.'

But the philosophy of her convictions did not prevent her wanting him to speak of her love and of her fear that in his reserve and silence he would escape her.

She lingered as long as she dared at the table, but after a while the conversation flagged and she knew that he wished to go.

Reluctantly, with the wistful resignation of a child who is taken from the theatre before the final scene in a pantomime, she rose to her feet and slowly passed through the door which he held open for her.

Outside, he said good-night, and there was a finality about him which checked the question on her lips of where he was going and how long he would be gone.

She went to her bed-room, telling herself she would settle down seriously to read the manuscripts that Hans had left behind him.

But when she was alone she did not go at once to the writing-table, but first to the looking-glass, to see how changed she was by this love she heralded within herself.

Her eyes were shining and her lips were parted by the breath which came between them.

'It is stifling in here,' Pamela thought, moving towards the window.

She remembered how Ion had said that a proof of the fourth dimension being in a more rarefied atmosphere was to be found in the desire for air evinced by all those who are either spiritual adventurers or of great intellectual development.

"Look how Messiahs and all great men seek the mountains," he had said. "Dreamers, poets, and geniuses cannot survive except in the country. Only people of little intelligence can exist for long in cities, or breathe with comfort the fetid atmosphere of restaurants and night-clubs. The air of inspiration and divinity is rarefied."

Pamela united in her mind divinity and love, thinking that they were, in reality and truth, indivisible.

Because of this love, she could not herself draw enough energy from the air, but must feel weak, as if her body could hardly support the surging of her spirit.

"Bruce," she whispered.

His name was precious to her, even as a mother will croon over the name of her child, choosing it because it holds some harmony with her mind beyond all others.

Presently Pamela made herself sit at the table and take up the pile of papers, discarding or retaining as she read them until they were sorted and arranged.

Somewhere far away in the house a clock struck twelve, and although her work was not finished she decided that it was too late and she would not continue further that night.

She undressed, crept under the mosquito-net, and once more the full flood of her love returned to her, and she wondered where Bruce was.

If he had returned, he would be sleeping farther along the passage, his eyes closed, his face at peace and young as when he was still a boy.

She saw her vision of him so clearly that she felt as if she could reach out her hand and touch his hair where it waved away from his forehead.

She would have done so in her thoughts had not a sound at her door recalled her attention.

The handle turned, and when she would have

cried out she found that her voice died in her throat
and to speak was impossible.

She lay stricken with fear as the door slowly
swung inwards.

'Why did I not lock it?' she thought to herself.

Then as a dark figure entered she was agonized
by that horror which is like some nightmare from
which the dreamer cannot escape.

She felt as though her body were paralysed, and
she watched the figure, which she could but faintly
see silhouetted against the open window, move towards the writing-table.

Then there was the faint glow of an electric torch.

Still Pamela could not move, and she knew that
the man who had entered was in Arab dress.

He was going to turn towards her, she thought,
and, anticipating that at any moment the torch might
shine on her face, sheer terror of what she might
see or of what might happen made her close her eyes.

She heard his stealthy movements, and even while
she shrank, thinking that perhaps death might come
to her in the form of a knife, there was the faint click
of her door closing.

Her eyes opened, and she knew that once again
she was alone, but for some moments she lay still,
hardly daring to breathe, tense and listening.

Panic made her spring from her bed with a sudden bound.

She rushed to the door and tore it open, trying
to cry out, to call for help; but her voice was strangled
in her constricted throat and the only sounds she
made were gasping and uncertain.

The passage was deserted, and without looking
round and without hesitation she ran down it towards Bruce's room.

She banged on his door with her hands, calling

his name in a hoarse whisper broken by sobbing breaths.

When he opened the door and she rushed towards him, clinging to him, holding to him with a terror which was utterly uncontrolled, all she could do was say his name over and over again.

"My dear," he said. "What is it? What has happened?"

He put his arms round her so that she could hide her face against his shoulder and still the pulsating tremor of her breasts against him.

"What is it?" he asked again, and then she felt his hands, and knew she had found security.

He calmed her so that her fear fell away as if it were a garment she discarded, her panic subsided, and she came again to a great quiet because she was in his arms.

*   *   *

"I love you," Pamela said.

The words fell between them not suddenly but as the blossoming of something perfect and complete.

It was not Bruce's arms round her that united them, but that they were one, indivisible each from the other.

He did not speak or kiss her, only held her closer to him, and looking into his face she needed no words to tell her that he was hers even as she was his.

They stood wrapped in a glory which was beyond them even while it came from within them, and the wonder of that moment was too intense for conscious thought.

"I love . . . you," Pamela whispered again.

This time her voice broke on the words, as if

mortality could not stand against the strain of them, could not transmit their beauty and their strength.

"You will catch cold," Bruce said very gently, his voice low even as hers had been.

He spoke as if he had come down to natural things from a great height and could not yet focus voice or attention.

His words dispersed none of the tension between them, only intensified their awareness of each other.

As he took up a silk dressing-gown which lay across a nearby chair and wrapped it round her shoulders, Pamela felt that he encompassed her with his love and that his gown was an armour.

Now in the movement which separated them for an instant, she remembered, far away, as though in some past time already half-forgotten, why she had come to the room.

She told him of the man who had entered her bed-room and of her fear which had kept her silent till in terror she had escaped.

"I will go and look," Bruce said; but she would not let him leave her.

"I am afraid," she said.

But she knew that in reality she could not bear to be parted from him.

"The thief may have stolen something," Bruce insisted.

"What?" Pamela asked. "I have no jewellery, and my money is locked away in the suitcase."

"You say that he looked only at the writing-table?" Bruce asked.

"There was nothing there of value," Pamela said. Then she exclaimed:

"Except the manuscripts I had been reading! That is what he came for."

"It is quite likely," Bruce said reflectively. "The description of Schaeffer's death has been in every paper, giving this address. His enemies, the Nazis, or whoever they may be, could easily bribe one of the servants, who would have known where his papers had been left.

"But I must go and make enquiries," he insisted. "Will you wait here? I will not be longer than I can help."

Against her inclination, she was forced to let him go.

When she was alone, Pamela sat and looked round the room, at everything that belonged to Bruce.

She wanted to touch the chairs on which he had sat and the pillows where he had rested his head, and to look into the mirrors, feeling that she would see no reflection of herself but of him.

It was a large room; the bed stood in an alcove, and the windows, wide open, looked over the court-yard.

Presently Pamela fastened the dressing-gown securely round her, realising for the first time that she had come to Bruce clad only in the transparency of her nightgown.

She felt no embarrassment, for her love made her capable only of a complete surrender of herself, which made her utterly his.

When she had moved about the room she sat on the low sofa before the window and waited. She could not think, only listen.

When would he return?

How soon would she see him again?

At last, after what seemed a long time, she heard his footsteps outside the door.

But when he entered, the questions she had meant to ask him were forgotten, and she could only look at him as her whole soul and heart poured out her love.

He seemed to her no ordinary man entering a room, but a god, and she would as easily have knelt to him as hold out her arms.

"There is no trace of the fellow," he said; "but all the papers have been taken from your room. I have made enquiries, but I feel that that is the last we shall hear of those manuscripts."

After he had spoken he fell silent, standing still, looking down at her until at last, yielding to the pressure of her hands, he sat down.

Woman-like, although she knew that he loved her, she wanted now to hear the words and watch them move his lips. She said:

"When did you first know?"

He understood, and replied:

"The first moment that I saw you."

"That night in the passage?" she questioned.

"At the first sound of your voice," he said; then added, "And when I saw your face, I was sure."

"Why did you not tell me?" she cried, regretting, as a lover always must, the time passed when love has been unexpressed.

"I should never have told you," Bruce said, and Pamela cried out as though he had hurt her.

"But why not?" she asked, suddenly afraid. "Would you have gone away, have let me go, without speaking?"

"Yes."

She had nothing to say, not even in reproach, for his words were a shock, and she sat staring at him with a bewildered expression on her face.

"But you do ... love me?" she asked at last, not because she doubted but because she was trying to grope her way back to some security.

"I love you," he repeated.

His words flamed into joy her whole being, so that she felt as if she were transfigured, and the vision of all she had ever dreamed, hoped, and longed for encompassed her.

"In books," Bruce said, "and even in life, men say: 'You are the woman I have waited for all my life.' But of us it is not true."

He paused, as if choosing his words, then went on:

"I think that the image of you has been with me always, and finding you has but made it real, substantiated it, but I have not waited for you or sought you, and now that you have come to me it is impossible that our unity can affect or alter what must be."

"And what is that?" Pamela asked.

He did not answer her but rose and went to the window, as if from the night outside he would seek not words to express himself but a relief from that proximity with her, which was disturbing all that had seemed static within him.

She did not understand what was happening; she could not as yet feel any great foreboding, for the joy of her own knowledge that she loved him was too great for her to admit anything else.

It filled her consciousness, her body, and her heart, to the exclusion even of fear or desire. She felt complete; they were one; there was nothing else she could want or ask for.

Looking at his back, the shape of his shoulders, and his head silhouetted against the night, she felt that overwhelming tenderness, that enfolding of love that comes from the deepest maternal instinct of a woman.

It was what she would feel for a child feeding at her breast, or for a man hurt or injured in body or mind.

She would pillow him against her, encradle him from all that was disturbing or adverse, and in her complete selflessness would comfort and protect him.

"Bruce," she called.

When he turned, she held out her arms in that wide gesture radiating all that she would give him.

Compelled, he drew nearer to her; but when he had come to the sofa he fell to his knees and hid his face against her.

Then, feeling the heaviness of him against her breast, the touch of his hair against her mouth, she knew in that moment a reserve of strength which all women have, and which makes them at such times more stalwart, more fierce, than a physically superior man.

A woman's strength is the miracle of a holy relic carried to war, against which power the weapons of an opposing Army cannot prevail.

"Tell me," she said gently.

She knew that she must share that pain which racked him, yet still she was unafraid, feeling that nothing could be too great for her to conquer, nothing too bad but that some healing quality in herself could relieve it.

When he raised his face from where it had lain hidden, he was very pale, and his eyes and mouth were those of a man who suffers agony.

"Why did this have to happen?" he said.

The words burst from him not as a question but as a protest, ringing to the far gate of heaven as one who cries from the depths of hell.

"I came to seek you," Pamela said. "It was a command."

"A command?" he asked. "From whom?"

Even as he spoke he knew the answer, and so she

did not reply, but put out her hands to touch him, not to gratify herself but as though they held some healing which could calm and quiet him.

"Shall I start at the very beginning?" he asked.

In his voice was the expression of one who seeks words for a story so poignant and so real that they unfold not a history but some inner nakedness.

"Tell me everything," Pamela answered. "From the very beginning."

She thought how she wished to know not only what he could remember but more: of his childhood, when he was a baby too small for thought.

As a small boy looking out at the world with eyes which judged those things grown too familiar to older people for comment—for to a child normality is ever a surprise until the passing years make him unresponsive.

'As a schoolboy,' Pamela thought, 'Bruce would have been very like he is now, but without, perhaps, that surety and determination which are so deeply characteristic of him.'

He would still have walked on tiptoe in an unknown world, seeking adventure at every corner, knowing the true joy of anticipation.

Only as age brings disillusionment do men and women know that obstacles do not vanish and that the conquest of them cannot be made in an instant.

Bruce's life was like a long road unfolding itself over the years, dipping and rising until it reached the point at which she stood; she half-turned to look back into the past, and waited for him to draw aside the veil which held its secret.

"I was born in India," Bruce began, "and my father held various administrative posts under the Government until, when I was seven years old, he became the British Agent at Gyantsé in Tibet.

"After the Younghusband expedition in 1904, the English were allowed the privilege of keeping a station there, although they could pass no farther into the country.

"Some months of each year my mother and I spent there, and when it was too cold, or frequently when it was too dangerous, we retired to Sikkim, where we had permission from the Maharajah to build a small house at the foot of the main pass over the Himalayas.

"I was brought up there among strange people and I grew to love and understand them even as you in your Scottish home knew and understood the crofters and gillies.

"After a few years my father came back to England and I was sent to an ordinary public school; but the impression I had gained in my early childhood could not be eradicated even by the normality of an ordinary boy's existence among boys.

"I enjoyed the games, even the lessons I found interesting, and my first term passed uneventfully, as did the holidays at the house my father and mother had taken in the country.

"Then one day came what I know now was a crystallisation of all that had been growing up and working within me, even though I did not realise it.

"I was summoned to the Housemaster's room, for some reason connected with the school—I have forgotten what it was—and when I went in he was absent.

"I stood looking round me, shuffling my feet, I expect, and not a little anxious in my mind as to what he required of me; then I started to look at the many books which filled the whole room.

"He was a scholar and a man known and respected outside the school for his learning. Something in the books magnetised me, so that, hardly aware of what I did, or else I should have been afraid, I took one down from the shelf.

"I held it in my hands, feeling that it contained some secret which must be mine at any cost. When I opened the volume I saw that the writing within was in Greek, so that I could not understand it.

"I had not taken the classical side at school. It was my father's decision that I should go into the Army, and as such, Latin and Greek were unimportant.

"But in those moments when I stood holding the book, a revelation came to my mind that here, in this unknown writing, was all that I sought and wished for in life. I did not turn over the pages, but stared at the place at which the book was opened.

"My Housemaster entered and looked surprised at what must have seemed to him for a moment an unpardonable impertinence.

"Then before he could speak I said to him:

" 'I have got to learn this language, Sir. Can I start at once?'

"Something in my earnestness, in the strangeness, perhaps, of my voice or expression, made him check any rebuke he was about to make. Instead, he invited me to sit and talk to him.

"When we had finished, he agreed to write to my father, and I myself went from his room to send pages of appeal, not only to change the course of my present education but to request that I might have extra lessons and special classes.

"My parents must have been a little sceptical of my enthusiasm, but they let me have my way, and during the holidays they began to realise that I was in earnest, for I could hardly be enticed away from my books, driven to conquer ignorance by a force which I did not even understand.

"I worked like a madman in the years that followed, and finally I not only made up for the years I had missed, but I took a scholarship to Oxford.

"There I continued, until I was offered a Professorship of the University, but when I understood the classical languages I turned to the modern, including the native dialects of India, Japan, and China.

"Still I did not know why I was driven by this desire. Then an invitation came to me quite unexpectedly to go to India and visit Sikkim, where I had lived as a child. I went, and what I found there changed the whole course of my life.

"I am telling you this," Bruce said, "so badly that I am not making clear even to myself the sequence of events which led up to what I am today. Perhaps the hardest thing in the world is for a man to make a comprehensive story of his own life.

"I want to make it real for you, and yet I feel that I am speaking so stupidly that it doesn't seem real even to myself."

"Go on," Pamela said. "I want to know everything, and I am trying to understand."

"It is hard now," Bruce continued, "to realise that when I took the journey to Sikkim I had no particular reason for going, save an interest in the land I had once known, and the idea that I needed a holiday.

"I had not then decided definitely upon my future; the question had arisen once or twice, but I had enough money to continue my studies, for my father was comparatively well off, and I was his only son.

"Now, telling the story to you, I see how lucky I have been, and yet I suppose luck is but another word for fate, or, if you prefer it, a pattern underlying all our lives so that no action, however trivial, is without meaning, and no opportunity presents itself until we are ready to grasp it."

He took Pamela's hand in his and looked at it as if he could find there some answer to the trouble which she heard in his voice.

As her fingers curled round his, as she responded to his touch, he looked up and met her eyes.

Then his control, overpowered by what could no longer be denied, broke, and he took her into his arms and kissed her lips.

She felt a streak like lightning flash through her and a wonder like a wave rise through her body.

It swept through her breasts and into her throat and was so ecstatic and wonderful that she knew that he carried her up into the sky and she touched the stars.

'This is the love which belongs to God,' she thought.

THE WISDOM OF THE VISHNU PURANA

She is Language; he is Thought.
She is Prudence; he is Law.
He is Reason; she is Sense.
She is Duty; he is Right.
He is Will; she is Wish.
He is Pity; she is Gift.
He is Song; she is Note.
She is Fuel; he is Fire.
She is Glory; he is Sun.
She is Motion; he is Wind.
He is Owner; she is Wealth.
He is Battle; she is Might.
He is Lamp; she is Light.
He is Day; she is Night.
He is Justice; she is Pity.
He is Channel; she is River.
She is Beauty; he is Strength.
She is Body; he is Soul.

—*The Union of Man and Woman*

Chapter Nine

"So, as I have told you, I am awaiting instructions."

Bruce finished his story, but his voice seemed to Pamela to go echoing on in the shadows of the room.

He had spoken for a long time. And she, sitting with her fingers interlaced together, with her eyes staring unseeingly out into the darkness of the night, felt as though she could not grasp all he had told her, could not understand.

It was fantastic, unreal; this could not be happening to her.

It could not be true that in the greatest and most wonderful moment of her life her happiness should be caught away from her, to leave her utterly forsaken and bereft.

Between Bruce and herself there was now this gulf, and she had no hope that it could be bridged by words or supplication.

Her love for him needed no expression, he knew that, and because of her upbringing by a scholar and among scholars, she knew more vividly than the average girl could have done how vital were these instructions for which Bruce was waiting.

She saw vividly how all his life had led to this culminating point, how his training and his interests were merged together to make him ready and sufficient for this.

How could love turn aside a man intent on what was not only his chosen career but also the most stupendous moment of it?

Before him there lay possibilities of which he could not even anticipate the magnitude.

Bruce had spoken in a voice which vibrated when he had described his first introduction to the Monasteries of Sikkim.

He told how he had furthered his acquaintance with the monks and Lamas until gradually he had been allowed to handle the sacred books which lie before the altar in every Buddhist Temple.

They are often unread, in many cases written in a language unknown to the monks who tend them, yet worshipped daily by the faithful.

It is the wisdom that they venerate, lying between the carved wooden or iron covers.

All who enter the Temple will prostrate themselves, and burn incense or light lamps in token not only of reverence but in the hope that one day, perhaps in another incarnation, they will be capable of reading and understanding the words of holiness.

These books, housed in every Monastery, are of great interest to those who seek faith, and to historians they are of inestimable value.

In the religion of a country, especially in the countries of the East, lies the tale of progress and the story of development.

It took Bruce years to gain their confidence, but gradually among the Lamas who guarded these treasures he had made many friends, so that he was allowed during his frequent visits to enter the more sacred parts of the Monasteries.

As his association with the Monasteries grew closer, he studied for a time under the Grand Lama, entering the Monastery as monk as well as pupil.

A Buddhist can become a monk at will; he makes no lifelong vows, and he gives his service to his Master only so long as he desires to do so.

He cannot be initiated into higher things or attain a sacred office unless he has resolved to dedicate his whole life; uninitiated, he is a free man.

There is no virtue in lip-service; there is no sense in that religion which gives a man the appearance of holiness if his thoughts and feelings are otherwise inclined.

There can be no conscription to God, only a willing surrender.

Bruce found inspiration for himself as well as for his intellect in the weeks he spent in the Monasteries.

Then on his last visit there came to him an offer which was so amazing that at first he was incredulous, unable to believe his good fortune.

The ancient religion of Tibet, before Buddhism was introduced into the country, was a weird one, yet by no means primitive, and its adherents are to this day called Bönpas.

They were Shamanists, who are sorcerers, magicians, and expert occultists, but little is known of them until, in the seventh century, their king, Srong btsam Gampo, sent learned men to Nepal and Kashmir to seek an alphabet so that the Buddhist writings might be translated.

For years it has been the theory of experts that, until the seventh century, there were no writings of the Bönpas.

But they themselves had declared through the centuries that there were in existence sacred books long before the reign of Srong btsam Gampo.

However, a certain Monastery on the Tibetan side of the Himalayas was always reputed to boast that in their possession were such writings.

No-one knew for certain, and it seemed unlikely that anyone would ever be able to prove the point one way or the other, for the Monastery in question was one of the most jealously guarded in Tibet.

Visitors were not allowed in the Temple, and on the rare occasion of their visits they were strictly excluded to an outer courtyard and guest-house.

By a strange chance, one of those coincidences which change not only the life of an individual but the whole stream of circumstance for all time, Bruce was able to do the Grand Lama of the Monastery a kindness.

They became friends, and the friendship ripened into real affection between the two.

At last Bruce, greatly daring, told the Lama of his desire to prove the authenticity of the Bönpas' claim to antiquity.

Instead of dismissing him with displeasure and a horrified refusal, the Grand Lama answered that he himself was not sure if the moment had not come when the history of Tibet, with its great past and the glory of its religion, should be given to the new generation and to the world outside.

Bruce could hardly believe his ears. This was more than he had dared to hope for, more than he had dared to anticipate even in his wildest dreams.

He waited for a long time for the decision not only of the Grand Lama himself but of the other learned men with whom he must consult before finally concluding what was best and wisest.

Eventually they agreed that Bruce should have the opportunity of handling and translating those works so sacred that for centuries no man had been permitted to study them.

Then he learnt to his surprise, that the writings were not, as everyone believed, kept in the Monastery itself, but were hidden in an even more sacred and inaccessible place, of which only a few chosen initiates knew the secret.

He was to be taken there, they promised him, and kept in comfort and security, but he would not be allowed to reveal to anyone his whereabouts.

He must trust himself utterly in the hands of those chosen as guides and guardians, and he must sever all links with the outside world, for no-one would be allowed to communicate with him.

Bruce would have agreed to any condition, and, knowing what he did of the Eastern character and the closely guarded secrets of which Western people seldom hear even a whisper, he was not surprised at the terms.

He came back to England, said good-bye to his friends, settled his estate, and without ties of any sort or kind set off for Tunis, where he had been told he would receive instructions as to how to proceed further.

He had no doubt that the way chosen for him would be as difficult and complicated as possible, so that when he finally reached the Monastery or Temple, he would be as vague and ignorant of where it was situated as he was at the present moment.

He was content, however, to lay his fate in the hands of the men he had grown to trust in the many years he had associated with them.

He knew that the precautions were no insult to himself but were taken from a sense of responsibility.

How long he would be lost to the world he had no idea. He was quite convinced that the work before him would take the lifetime of not one but many men, if it was to be correctly and conscientiously handled.

"I may remain away, ten, twenty, perhaps thirty

years," he said to Pamela. "I know a little about the
Tibetan libraries—they are completely uncatalogued,
collected together without any method.

"The treasures of every generation, accumulated
in one place until the brain reels at such a super-
abundance of wealth. I believe I shall find awaiting
me writings of such value and such wonder that all
the histories of the world may have to be altered
because of what they reveal."

He sighed as he continued:

"It is more than likely that long before I can
start on any translations or transcriptions, I must
spend years in acquainting myself with what is
there, and trying to find some sort of order in the
midst of chaos."

Every word that he spoke brought home to
Pamela more and more clearly how hopeless it was
for her to nourish any hope in her heart that there
might be a future for them together.

Bruce's whole life must be given completely and
absolutely to what lay before him.

How could he, in the circumstances, ask or expect any woman to wait for him? She knew that to
himself such an idea would be impossible.

What he was about to do set him apart from her
as completely as though he took the vows of Catholic
priesthood.

Already he had given his word, and this meeting
with her was but a parting glance at the world he
must leave behind.

Yet it was hard; the agony of it seemed to pierce
her so that it was with difficulty that she prevented
herself from crying out aloud, from pleading with
him, from falling on her knees in supplication that
he might stay with her a little longer.

There was a quiet in the room; outside, there was that silence before sunrise when human vibrations are still and the earth gathers to her bosom her strength, ready to give birth to a new day.

Soon, swiftly, without prelude and without twilight, the dawn would come, a burst of Eastern glory.

Pamela knew that it would bring to her a fleeting, false hope, and in the sunshine she would think: 'There must be some way out. There must be some way that I can hold him, so that our love need not die.'

But when she turned her face towards Bruce she saw that he was drawn and pale.

What he had said had taken its toll of him, and the influx of tenderness she felt made her wish to comfort him rather than herself, for true love must ever be generous, always anxious to give.

There were no words with which they could bridge that farewell which already lay between them. They were as two ships passing in an ocean, carried each moment farther and farther away from each the other into the vast loneliness of empty horizons.

While she yearned towards him, while she would have given her hope of heaven and her future years on earth for the promise of but a short time more in his arms, like fate there came a knock on the door.

When Bruce opened it, he found a messenger bearing a sealed letter.

Pamela knew what it contained, and she hid her face as if even the opening of the envelope was a knife which stabbed her, and she could not watch her own death sentence.

"I am to go to a certain house in an oasis about thirty miles south of Tunis," Bruce said. "Horses and camels will be ready for me at dawn."

There was no elation in his voice, only the deep determination of one who will do his duty whatever the cost may be.

"Let me go with you," Pamela pleaded. "Let me be with you just these last hours. It is not much to ask, Bruce, thirty miles together out of a lifetime we must spend apart. Please let me."

When he would have hesitated she rose and went to him, lifting up her arms to his shoulders and looking into his face, so that because of the love he felt for her he could deny her nothing.

Although he was doubtful of the wisdom of what she suggested, she overruled by the tenderness of her lips anything he might have said.

There was now no passion in the kiss, but the clinging together as of two children finding comfort in the closeness of companionship.

When Bruce had kissed her eyes and the softness of her hair where it curled away from her white forehead, he said gently:

"You must go and dress, my love."

She obeyed him and turned towards the door, but before she could reach it, instinctively they drew together again, clinging one to the other in an agony.

Long before she was dressed, the sun was shining golden and brilliant.

But the slant of the shadows left the little courtyard in darkness, and to Pamela the sound of the fountain was like the trickle of desolate tears.

She looked round at her bed-room. She seemed to have grown immeasurably older since she had last left it, to have lived a whole lifetime of emotion, to have ranged the whole octave from happiness to ecstasy, and from ecstasy to despair.

In one night she had blossomed through love to womanhood.

Far behind her she had left the last remnant of a girl who had not known but who had wanted love. Now it had come, and with it hand in hand had been the shrouded figure of despair.

As she dressed, Pamela packed, for she was determined that whatever happened she would not return to this Hotel where she had found all that she sought for one brief instant before it left her again.

She remembered a picture she had once seen many years ago hanging in an unfrequented, little-known gallery.

It had been of a man clutching with outstretched hands at an eagle rising away from him in flight; he fell backwards, eluded, his hand holding but one feather of the great majestic bird soaring into the vastness and beauty of the sky.

To her that eagle symbolised love. So it would pass from her as she barely heard the flutter of its wings or knew the majesty and wonder of it.

When it was gone, she would be left only with the feather of memory.

Here, in this room, where she had known the sorrow of Hans's death, the terror of physical fear, and the dawn of a great love, she stood a pilgrim, ready to set forth, but without hope and without desire.

'When I leave these four walls,' Pamela thought, 'there is nothing more to come.'

Yet, as an answer to her despondency, came in an instant the high, resonant note of the Moslems, calling all Islam to prayer, and she fell on her knees beside the window as she had done the night Hans died.

But when she would have prayed, she could find nothing in her heart save a throbbing misery, from which she shrank, afraid that the very vastness of it might overwhelm her.

'I must pray for little things,' she thought.

She tried to concentrate on the small matters of life, for quite clearly she knew that they were the arms which would bear her through the future, the hands which would comfort her and give her new courage.

And in the little things of life, as in the morning of the day to come, she would know that "Allah is great, Allah is good."

*   *   *

As they paced slowly over the sand the camels grunted as though in protest against their lot of being continually on the move for some unknown destination.

There is a dignity about camels in spite of their uncouth appearance; their reserve is matched only by the majesty of the Sphinx.

What they think and what they feel has never yet been known to man.

A camel-ride is not a comfortable way of travel, and Pamela was glad that she had been provided with a horse, a fine animal with the arched neck and sensitive nostrils which showed Arabian strain.

Bruce rode a black mare; the camels carried the luggage and their guide, who in flowing white robes had been waiting for them outside the House of the Star.

Three other attendants were provided in this escort, which had come bearing instructions for Bruce but with no other information for the travellers.

He asked one or two questions, and then, realising that they were unwelcome, was wise enough to say no more and to proceed on the first part of his journey with the same unquestioning obedience which he knew would be required of him later.

Pamela was more curious, not from any idle interest, but because anything and everything that Bruce did was of interest to her.

She wanted to store away a lifetime of memories so that in the years to come she could imagine him from babyhood to man, and through manhood to the recluse in some high Himalayan Lamasery from which she felt he would never emerge.

She knew that he must go, she knew that any arguments she might offer could in no way deter him from his chosen course.

In her mind she acknowledged that he was right, but her body cried out against this sacrifice of themselves, this turning away from the revelation of a love so great and so deep that she felt it must always have been waiting for them.

'There is no reason in love,' she thought.

She imagined the superciliously raised eye-brows and the comments of those who did not understand that in a conventional acquaintanceship of a few hours, a lifetime of emotion could take place.

It was impossible to say, "I met Bruce two days ago," or, "I have known him so many hours."

Always she had known him, always she had within herself been moving towards this realisation of unity.

Everything and every person in her life had been but a rung in the ladder which eventually led her to the moment when she had encountered this man.

She had not met him merely by coming with

Hans to Tunis, or by leaving Cowton Hall for Bugalé, or through her meeting with Arthur.

In her childhood, her development, her education, and the departure of her family from Scotland were steps, not even then the first steps, towards the man she must love.

Bruce knew that in Pamela he had found for himself the woman whom every man idealises from the moment that in his mother he senses and learns of the ideal woman.

Men have been called hunters, but actually they are seekers, ever searching for an ideal.

Every man, lonely without his companion, until he finds the one woman who can satisfy and hold him, must continue to pass searching through the world, following many false trails, but true in his heart to that beauty of womanhood, from which he can never escape.

For that aspiration born within men when they first lie cradled in a woman's arms, they must seek until they attain.

Bruce's mother was dead, but he told Pamela how much she had meant to him throughout his life, and except for the love of a man for the woman who is his own, there is no stronger tie than that between mother and son.

"She was so understanding," Bruce said. "I think there were few secrets between us. Often I would resolve to myself that I would keep something back from her, perhaps afraid of hurting her or distressing her by something I had done or intended to do.

"But always when we were together, when she came as she often did to say good-night to me, sitting beside my bed, never asking a confidence but ready to receive one, I would find myself, almost without meaning to, telling her what I had intended to keep secret."

"If your mother were alive today," Pamela asked in a low voice, "would you have accepted this expedition?"

She was almost ashamed of her question, yet she could not help that deep pang of jealousy which made her feel that perhaps this other woman who had meant so much in Bruce's life might have had the power to hold him.

Bruce was a long time in answering; she felt the movement of the horse beneath her, heard the jingle of the harness, and smelt the sharp warm tang of the animals, mixed with the strange, exotic breath of the desert.

"I know," Bruce said at last, as though before he spoke he had been delving deep for the truth, "that my mother would have sent me on this mission. She knew even in the early days that my work was a preparation, though for what neither of us was quite certain, but she believed absolutely in a God who, all-foreseeing and of perfect wisdom, controls and directs our lives.

"In all her troubles—and she had many in her life—as in her smallest difficulties, she was content to believe that everything was for the best.

"She personally had never known what appeared to be an evil through which ultimately had not come good. Her faith was simple, direct, and very real to her.

"Perhaps that is why all my life I have been content not to worry for the future but to concentrate on the present, knowing that what I do today will be harvested in some form tomorrow."

In Bruce's eyes was the light of a visionary, and

Pamela felt that he rose in such faith to heights far beyond the narrow pilgrim path she herself trod.

But when she would have felt humble, Bruce put out his hand and took hers; instantly a tide of joy flooded over her, so that she was conscious of nothing save the fact that they were linked together, riding towards a horizon where sea and sky mingled in an indefinable line.

Every minute, she knew, took them nearer to that severance, in which she could not yet believe because it was too vast a misery for her comprehension.

Occasionally they would see other travellers in the distance, moving across the sand; each time a fantastic hope would spring to Pamela's mind that perhaps here was a messenger coming to save her even at this last hour, bringing tidings which would release Bruce from his given word.

After a time the sun grew so hot that she covered her head and wore dark glasses. Even so, she felt the scorching rays, and she was glad when at noon they halted in the shade of a few palm trees for food and rest.

After they had eaten, they lay back on the woollen rugs and cushions which had been provided for them.

They looked back over the distance they had come to where the roofs of Tunis stood faintly against the sky-line, shimmering silver in the hot sun like some mirage which might vanish at any moment from their sight.

"It is all so strange," Pamela said, "so unexpected, and yet with you I feel that nothing outside us could be of any importance, nothing could disturb or frighten me. It is as if you and I are complete, apart from the world, and immune, when we are together, from everybody."

"And this our Eden?" Bruce asked with a smile. "It is like a little desert island. I wonder, would you get bored?"

But he knew the answer to his question even as he asked it, for he read in Pamela's eyes complete surrender to himself.

Their glances met, and as they did so the blood of each quickened; a tension held them both while their hearts throbbed, and the tremor of deep desire seized and held them spellbound.

"You are lovely," Bruce said.

His words brought the blood flowing into Pamela's cheeks, and only the presence of the servants waiting beside the camels kept her from his arms.

Bruce raised her hand to his lips and kissed it lingeringly, touching each finger and the palm.

"If only this could never end," Pamela whispered.

Although it was with a smile that he answered, there was a sadness in his eyes.

Then, because they could not bear to speak too intimately of themselves, Pamela asked him to tell her something of the Lamas.

He began to speak of their vast Monasteries, housing five or six thousand monks, built high into the face of the mountains, reached only by narrow and perilous yak-paths, by which they must obtain their supplies and make contact with the outer world.

"There is a deep peace in such places," Bruce said. "I cannot explain it, but it is as if one becomes fused into a new plan of existence. The world sinks in introspection into something so infinitesimal and unimportant that it is only with an effort that one can remember familiar things.

"The voices raised at prayer, voices made mellow and beautiful through years of practised breathing, give an indefinable thrill which no opera or orchestra can ever inspire."

He told her of the turquoise-tiled roofs, of great pagodas covered in real gold, of Temple towers carved and inlaid with ivory.

And of the crimson robes of the monks themselves, worn by time and weather into every conceivable shade of red, so that one gasped at the colour when, as a flowing tide, they assembled for prayer, thousands of them, in the great courtyards.

Pamela was envious of Bruce, for in such strange yet beautiful surroundings he could escape much of the misery which she knew must be hers when she returned to the world and moved to the monotony of her familiar daily existence.

Then she spoke to him of Arthur, how much his security and steadfastness meant to her, and how once she had likened him to St. Joseph.

Bruce understood and made her promise that when he had left her she would go and find Arthur.

But as she made the promise Pamela felt the chill of saying "when you are gone," and she knew that in her farewell to him she would erect a mile-stone for all time, so that everything would become "before I met Bruce" or "after I met Bruce."

Nothing, she thought, could hurt or touch her after this; no longer would she be annoyed or irritated at home, and the atmosphere of Cowton would not seem suffocating, for the restless ambition which had made her resentful would be gone.

Instead, a calm tolerance would take its place as though in old age one should say:

"It does not matter, it is unimportant."

Only she knew that at night her whole being would cry out for Bruce, that then the little things with which she could fill her days would be of no use to her, and that in the darkness she must fight her worst and cruellest battles.

'If only I could have had a baby!' she thought to herself. 'If he could have given me that, so that some part of him would have remained with me, I could have found happiness in such a consummation of our love!'

But she knew that it would have been unfair; a child in its growing needs both father and mother, even as a flower to come to its blossoming needs the nurture of both earth and sky.

Yet Pamela, riding along, could not help but think of how she might have held in her arms a tiny replica of Bruce.

In her imagination she felt its head heavy against her breast, and she knew that tenderness which is in all women for the helplessness of their own flesh and blood.

Later she grew tired, for it was a long journey; the heat of the sun fatigued both men and beasts.

They went slowly because of the camels, and the afternoon drew on long before they were in sight of their destination; but Pamela was glad, for she was afraid of their journey's end.

Bruce, too, wondered what reception they might have, because without warning, and without permission, he had brought with him a companion.

After a while he spoke with the guide, and finally despatched him on ahead of the fastest camel, to say that they were approaching and that Pamela was with him.

When the man was gone, his white robes flowing

out behind him like the sails of a great ship, Bruce linked Pamela's hand in his, and they rode knee to knee in thankfulness that they still had a little while before them.

"When you think of me," Pamela said, "will you remember this moment rather than later, when my courage may fail me? I should like you to think of me as a companion riding beside you in all your voyages, wherever they may take you."

"That is where you will always be in my mind," he said—"always with me. In that way, we can never be separated."

"Tell me once again that you love me," Pamela said; "I want to hear you say the words."

"I love you with my whole heart and soul," he answered, and for a while she was content.

Soon they saw looming far ahead many trees, and in the midst of them the silhouette of a great white house with its roof against the sky.

Pamela knew that soon now would come their parting. Bruce's hand, still in hers, gave her courage, so that she would not show her fear, but turned towards him with a smile and said:

"It is like some enchanted palace, and very lovely."

Before they reached the place, the sun sank and instantly there was darkness, and a great star hung over the house as though it led them as the Wise Men had been led two thousand years before.

The camels, sensing that they were nearly home, moved forward quickly.

Pamela saw their guide coming towards them, returning to escort them on the last stages of their journey.

When he was within earshot he said in his own language:

"Allah is good! Allah is wise! The way is ended!"

And Bruce, as was courteous and traditional, answered:

"Allah is wise. Thanks be to Allah."

Then before them they saw the huge gateway leading into the courtyard open for them to enter.

THE WISDOM OF MANGALAM

Lead me from the unreal to the real
Lead me from darkness to light
Lead me from the mortal to the immortal.

—*Dattátreya*

Chapter Ten

O nce through the gateway, the small cavalcade of travellers entered a huge stone courtyard shaded by great palm trees and enclosed by white walls, from the windows of which shone many welcoming lights.

Dogs came bounding at the heels of servants who sprang foward to assist Pamela to alight, and then led her and Bruce towards another door which opened into the house.

Pamela's first impressions were vague, for she was agitated, and not a little afraid of her reception.

She was conscious that they walked through long, beautifully arched passages carpeted by thick and handsome rugs, and that there was an atmosphere of peace and the faint scent of sandalwood.

Then the servant who preceded them showed them into a large room furnished with embroidered hangings against which even an inexperienced eye could appreciate the beauty of antique and specimen furniture.

There was no-one in the room, but long windows opened onto yet another courtyard and there they perceived waiting for them two men.

There were trees, flowers, and a little stream which ran through the courtyard and vanished at the far end into the house itself.

But all this Pamela sensed rather than saw, for

she was concentrating on the men who advanced towards them.

The first was tall and dark, with a short beard, and she recognised his distinctive features immediately; he was a famous French philosopher, author, and explorer, of whom her father had often spoken and whose books she herself had read.

'This,' she thought, 'must be his home.'

She was not mistaken, for with outstretched hand he greeted both herself and Bruce, welcoming them with a courtesy which for a moment dispelled her shyness.

But when she turned to the other man she felt less assured. Of medium height, he wore the dark brown robes of a monk; his face, impassive and bearing the characteristics of Mongolian blood, was unlined and serene, yet there was an impression of age about him.

He bowed to her and then turned to Bruce with a smile of welcome. Bruce exclaimed in surprise and greeted him with affection and reverence.

"This, Pamela," he said, "is the Lama Tsawi Syong, who has been sent to me by the Grand Lama."

The two men spoke in a language unfamiliar to Pamela, but she saw the eagerness and the sense of excitement about Bruce which told her more clearly than any words that the arrangements for his departure were complete and ready.

Food and drink were brought by silently moving servants and set in the courtyard, which was diffused by some hidden lights, giving an air of elusive mystery to everything, and accentuated by the white walls of the house rising high on either side.

Chairs and couches were arranged on the stone floor, and books lay carelessly on one table as though their host spent much of his time here, making the courtyard both library and dining-room.

Out of politeness Pamela forced herself to eat some fruit and sip the wine which was set before her, but it was with an effort, for she felt the terror of the passing minutes and knew already that Bruce was moving away from her.

He was talking with the Lama, and in his attention she felt that she was already forgotten.

There was no reference made to her unexpected arrival, her host going out of his way to treat her like some honoured guest.

Yet she was tense in her misery and could hardly forbear to cry out and tell them of her agony.

The exotic surroundings, the little group they made under the trees, the scent of the flowers, and the excellent food and wine, were all in mockery of the misery that she was experiencing.

It was as if she took part in some elaborate drama, acting the leading rôle upon the stage, when/ her heart was broken, her private life bereft of all that had meant happiness.

Once or twice in sheer desperation she gripped her hands together beneath the table to prevent the weakness of tears coming to her eyes, but though her words sometimes faltered, her pride kept her outwardly steadfast.

When they had finished eating, her host said:

"Perhaps you would like to see my garden. The moon has risen and it will be very lovely."

Pamela felt that he sympathised and was giving them a chance to be alone; she accepted the invitation, hoping that Bruce too would understand.

She looked at him with meaning, and he finished his conversation with the Lama and followed her towards an iron gate in the courtyard, beyond which lay the garden.

As they reached it, Pamela looked back and saw

the Lama standing as they had left him, still and expressionless, looking after them.

She shivered as one might who senses the power of something strong beyond understanding and mysterious beyond comprehension.

When they had entered the garden Pamela gasped for a moment at the loveliness of that which lay before them, for the moon rising over the trees revealed such perfection as she had not deemed it possible to find in the centre of a desert.

There were great branches weighed down by blossoms and fruit, and pools of deep water silver in the moonlight.

When he had invited them to wander as they would, their host turned towards the house and left them.

For a moment both were under the spell of his presence so that they could not come together.

At last, with a little cry, Pamela held out her arms, and the next moment her face was hidden in Bruce's shoulder.

When she could touch him, everything fell from her save the desire to love him and to capture happiness for a few brief moments.

She touched his face and his hair, lifting her lips to his until, inflamed by her and caught into a like ecstasy, he held her closer and closer, raining kisses upon her face and mouth till both were blinded with wonder.

"My dear love! My own! My darling," he murmured incoherently.

Pamela strained herself against him until it seemed that they were one, each part of the other.

It was their enchanted moment, and she wished wildly that she could die in this second while he held her, when in the moonlight in this magical garden she was utterly his and he was hers.

She would ask for nothing more, no future, not even for immortality, if she could pass into oblivion with his name on her lips and his arms round her.

"I love you," she murmured again and again.

It was as though the words were some talisman which could join them for eternity, a symbol, like a wedding-ring, of their union.

Then at last, when humanity could bear the fire of such passion no longer, when Pamela was near to fainting, she hid her face against his neck.

They stood locked together for a long time in stillness. At last, Bruce, his voice broken and low said:

"I have to leave you at dawn."

As he spoke, Pamela cried out like an animal that is caught cruelly in a trap from which it knows there is no escape.

"You know what it means to me," he said. "There is no need for words between us, my beloved, but it is of you I am thinking, and of your future."

Pamela checked the words he would have spoken.

"I am all right," she said bravely.

She raised her head to meet his eyes with a courage that amazed him.

"You will never regret this?" he asked gently.

It was as if he must hear her deny it in words, even while he knew within himself that it was impossible for her to blaspheme against their love.

In answer Pamela said:

"There are some words in Ion's book. They express so much better than I can what you mean to me. Listen, my darling."

In a low voice, leaning against his shoulder, the light of the moon falling on her face, she murmured:

> *"There can be no dividing of ourselves.*
> *You are of me, as I am part of you.*
> *And if our earthly paths uncrossed,*
> *Had left us unreflected, incomplete,*
> *In this brief life, what matter,*
> *When the future and the past are ever ours?"*

When she had finished speaking, when the sound of her voice had died away, her courage failed her.

Torn by terrible sobs, she covered her face with her hands and sank, helpless, at Bruce's feet.

When he would have raised her, for she was crouched, with bowed head, the thought came to him that she was like one of the women weeping at the foot of the Cross.

The agony of her tears, and the bitterness of seeing the woman he loved utterly broken at his feet, shattered the composure to which Bruce had steeled himself.

Into his face came a look of deep resignation. For a moment he looked up into the starry sky as one who prays for help and deliverance, or as one who asks forgiveness for what he is about to do; then he said:

"I can't bear it. I can't leave you. Nothing can be of importance beside this love, this miracle which God himself has given us."

Pamela heard him, but now nothing could check her tears, for her body could stand no further strain and must find relief from its misery.

"My darling," Bruce said, "listen to me. I leave to you the decision of what we must do. If you tell me to go on with what I have planned, to continue with this work which until now has seemed my duty and my privilege, I will obey you.

"If, on the other hand, you bid me stay, then I shall know that that choice is made by some power beyond ours, and I swear that whatever path you bid me take, to that will I keep, without regrets, and content because you have willed it."

Gently he touched Pamela's head so that she was stilled, and a great peace came to her from his words and his touch.

"But this I swear," Bruce said, as though he were taking an oath, "that I will love you forever, with the whole of my body and mind, whether I am with you or apart."

Pamela did not move, and after a minute he added:

"Will you come and tell me when you are ready? I will wait until you come."

When she was alone, Pamela crouched still lower, touching the grass with her fingers, feeling as if she drew strength and comfort from the bosom of the earth itself.

For a little while she could not think because her senses were weak with the fatigue of suffering, and her breath came uneasily through lips which quivered with the storm through which she had passed.

After a long time she rose and looked round her, seeking some sign which might guide her, some token by which she might know what she must do.

She knew that for love of her Bruce had offered a supreme sacrifice, for no man could do more than offer his life to the woman he loves. It is harder to give the years of living than the moment of dying.

She saw how their life together might be one of perfect happiness, saw the pattern that they might make of all they did, so that when they were old they could look back and see that the years had been unwasted, had been full of service to mankind.

Without Bruce she saw herself wandering alone in a mist unlit by the sunshine, yet even so she must carry within herself the light of perfect love, which was theirs, one for the other, together or apart.

And she felt that she could not bear such an existence, and that she must have Bruce with her.

'I will go and tell him,' she thought. 'He has sworn to stand by my decision, and he will not break his word, however much it costs him.'

She felt how she would love him more, in that she must forever keep from his mind any moment of regret. Her tenderness must be boundless, her sympathy and understanding infinite.

She turned towards the house, savouring for a moment the ecstasy she would know when she found Bruce again and there was no farewell between them.

But even as she turned, she knew that duty, as an angel with a flaming sword, stood before her, and she saw that Bruce must give to the world that which was required of him.

She knew that she, because of her need of him, could not prevent the fulfilment which had been ordained.

She fought against her conscience and her intuition, her heart rising against them, but weakly, as one who already recognises a victor and fights without the spirit of confidence.

"I cannot let him go, I can't," she whispered.

But all that was best and bravest in herself told her that she must.

Now she was past weeping. Her suffering in its intensity numbed her, and she knew what she must do, but yet she prayed with broken words for escape.

Slowly, as if in bondage to some force greater than her will, she moved towards the house, and as she came to the iron gate she saw that standing in the shadows waiting for her was the Lama.

She raised her head and looked at him; there was no need for explanations, for she felt that he already knew not only the decision to which she had come but of her trial and temptation.

There was an aura of power about him, as of a man controlled not from without but from within, so that he had in his mind attained that supremacy of self which is for all men's conquest, but was Adam's without trial, before sin.

Pamela, through dry lips and in a voice which she hardly recognised as her own, asked in a whisper:

"Where is Bruce?"

The Lama answered:

"He is in the courtyard."

Then Pamela said:

"I must speak to him and then I must go. I can't bear to wait and watch him leave me. Let me say good-bye, then I will return to Tunis."

"It shall be as you wish," the Lama answered. "There are horses ready now, and a guide shall escort you."

"Were you afraid that I would keep him?" she asked.

With a smile that illuminated his face with an almost unearthly radiance, the Lama replied:

"No."

When she looked at him, surprised at his certainty, he added:

"I knew that you would be worthy of his love."

Pamela felt the tears come to her eyes, and she said:

"You will look after him for me?"

"You will both be in God's keeping," the Lama answered, "and in our prayers."

She felt as if he had blessed her, but she could not thank him.

She turned and walked through the gateway into the courtyard. She moved slowly towards the centre where the couches and chairs were arranged.

The lights had been dimmed now that the moon had risen, and its light, unequalled by any light of artificial making, flowed over everything, turning the falling water into glittering diamonds and laying a silver sheen on the flowers.

Under the shadows cast by the branches and the leaves of the palm trees, Pamela could see Bruce lying on a couch.

Her heart beat and her hands trembled, but she held her head high in the strength and bravery of determination.

Then as she drew near to him she saw that he was asleep. For a moment she felt bitter that he could not have waited and kept awake to hear what she had to say.

But she saw that it was the sleep of utter fatigue, of a man worn out not by action but by emotion, and that there were lines of suffering under his eyes and beside his mouth.

She stood looking down at him, and she knew that it was best that they should part like this.

She dropped to her knees, and would have brushed his hand with her lips, but instead she found herself praying:

"God keep you, my darling. God give you strength and purpose. God protect you. I am yours now and for all eternity and ever ... The future and the past are ours."

Her voice broke, and without touching him she rose, and without looking at him again she walked towards the house.

In the great room a servant was waiting; he led her through the passage to the outer courtyard. Her horse was waiting, saddled, her guide was mounted by its side.

Without a word and without farewell, Pamela rode through the courtyard which led to the desert, and they turned their horses towards the north.

She saw in her imagination the road that they must take, and the sea beyond Tunis, and beyond that again the path back to England.

Tears ran unchecked down her cheeks and she tasted the salt of them on her mouth.

There was a long ride before them, but the moonlight made clear the way, so that she rode in the midst of light.

She thought that there would be no darkness because later would come the dawn.

THE WISDOM OF THE BHAGAVADGITA

"The Souls light shineth pure in every place;
And they who, by such eye of wisdom, see
How Matter, and what deals with it, divide;
And how the Spirit and the flesh have strife.
Those wise ones go the way which leads to Life!"

—*The Song Celestial*

ABOUT THE AUTHOR

BARBARA CARTLAND, the world's most famous romantic novelist, who is also an historian, playwright, lecturer, political speaker and television personality, has now written over 200 books. She has also had many historical works published and has written four autobiographies as well as the biographies of her mother and that of her brother Ronald Cartland, who was the first Member of Parliament to be killed in the last war. This book has a preface by Sir Winston Churchill. Barbara Cartland has sold 80 million books over the world, more than half of these in the U.S.A. She broke the world record in 1975 by writing twenty books, and her own record in 1976 with twenty-one. In private life, Barbara Cartland, who is a Dame of the Order of St. John of Jerusalem, has fought for better conditions and salaries for Midwives and Nurses. As President of the Royal College of Midwives (Hertfordshire Branch), she has been invested with the first Badge of Office ever given in Great Britain, which was subscribed to by the Midwives themselves. She has also championed-the-cause for old people and founded the first Romany Gypsy Camp in the world. Barbara Cartland is deeply interested in Vitamin Therapy and is President of the British National Association for Health.

BARBARA CARTLAND
PRESENTS
THE ANCIENT WISDOM SERIES

The world's all-time bestselling author of romantic fiction, Barbara Cartland, has established herself as High Priestess of Love in its purest and most traditionally romantic form.

"We have," she says, "in the last few years thrown out the spiritual aspect of love and concentrated only on the crudest and most debased sexual side.

"Love at its highest has inspired mankind since the beginning of time. Civilization's greatest pictures, music, prose and poetry have all been written under the influence of love. This love is what we all seek despite the temptations of the sensuous, the erotic, the violent and the perversions of pornography.

"I believe that for the young and the idealistic, my novels with their pure heroines and high ideals are a guide to happiness. Only by seeking the Divine Spark which exists in every human being, can we create a future built on the foundation of faith."

Barbara Cartland is also well known for her Library of Love, classic tales of romance, written by famous authors like Elinor Glyn and Ethel M. Dell, which have been personally selected and specially adapted for today's readers by Miss Cartland.

"These novels I have selected and edited for my 'Library of Love' are all stories with which the readers can identify themselves and also be assured that right will triumph in the end. These tales elevate and activate the mind rather than debase it as so many modern stories do."

Now, in August, Bantam presents the first four novels in a new Barbara Cartland Ancient Wisdom series. The books are THE FORBIDDEN CITY by Barbara Cartland, herself; THE ROMANCE OF TWO WORLDS by Marie Corelli; THE HOUSE OF FULFILLMENT by L. Adams Beck; and BLACK LIGHT by Talbot Mundy.

"Now I am introducing something which I think is of vital importance at this moment in history. Following my own autobiographical book I SEEK THE MIRACULOUS, which Dutton is publishing in hardcover this summer, I am offering those who seek 'the world behind the world' novels which contain, besides a fascinating story, the teaching of Ancient Wisdom.

"In the snow-covered vastnesses of the Himalayas, there are lamaseries filled with manuscripts which have been kept secret for century upon century. In the depths of the tropical jungles and the arid wastes of the deserts, there are also those who know the esoteric mysteries which few can understand.

"Yet some of their precious and sacred knowledge has been revealed to writers in the past. These books I have collected, edited and offer them to those who want to look beyond this greedy, grasping, materialistic world to find their own souls.

"I believe that Love, human and divine, is the jail-breaker of that prison of selfhood which confines and confuses us . . .

"I believe that for those who have attained enlightenment, super-normal (not super-human) powers are available to those who seek them."

All Barbara Cartland's own novels and her Library of Love are available in Bantam Books, wherever paperbacks are sold. Look for her Ancient Wisdom Series to be available in August.

Barbara Cartland

The world's bestselling author of romantic fiction. Her stories are always captivating tales of intrigue, adventure and love.

☐	2917	DREAM AND THE GLORY	$1.50
☐	10339	THE TAMING OF LADY LORINDA	$1.50
☐	10340	DISGRACEFUL DUKE	$1.50
☐	10341	VOTE FOR LOVE	$1.50
☐	10342	THE MYSTERIOUS MAID-SERVANT	$1.50
☐	10709	THE MAGIC OF LOVE	$1.50
☐	10710	KISS THE MOONLIGHT	$1.50
☐	10971	THE RHAPSODY OF LOVE	$1.50
☐	10715	THE MARQUIS WHO HATED WOMEN	$1.50
☐	10972	LOOK, LISTEN AND LOVE	$1.50
☐	10975	A DUEL WITH DESTINY	$1.50
☐	10976	CURSE OF THE CLAN	$1.50
☐	10977	PUNISHMENT OF A VIXEN	$1.50
☐	11101	THE OUTRAGEOUS LADY	$1.50
☐	11168	A TOUCH OF LOVE	$1.50
☐	11169	THE DRAGON AND THE PEARL	$1.50

Barbara Cartland

The world's bestselling author of romantic fiction. Her stories are always captivating tales of intrigue, adventure and love.

☐	11270	THE LOVE PIRATE	$1.50
☐	11271	THE TEMPTATION OF TORILLA	$1.50
☐	11372	LOVE AND THE LOATHSOME LEOPARD	$1.50
☐	11410	THE NAKED BATTLE	$1.50
☐	11512	THE HELL-CAT AND THE KING	$1.50
☐	11537	NO ESCAPE FROM LOVE	$1.50
☐	11580	THE CASTLE MADE FOR LOVE	$1.50
☐	11579	THE SIGN OF LOVE	$1.50
☐	11595	THE SAINT AND THE SINNER	$1.50
☐	11649	A FUGITIVE FROM LOVE	$1.50
☐	11797	THE TWISTS AND TURNS OF LOVE	$1.50
☐	11801	THE PROBLEMS OF LOVE	$1.50
☐	11751	LOVE LEAVES AT MIDNIGHT	$1.50
☐	11882	MAGIC OR MIRAGE	$1.50
☐	10712	LOVE LOCKED IN	$1.50
☐	11959	LORD RAVENSCAR'S REVENGE	$1.50

Buy them at your local bookstore or use this handy coupon:

Bantam Books, Inc., Dept. BC, 414 East Golf Road, Des Plaines, Ill. 60016

Please send me the books I have checked above. I am enclosing $_____
(please add 50¢ to cover postage and handling). Send check or money order—no cash or C.O.D.'s please.

Mr/Mrs/Miss_____

Address_____

City_____State/Zip_____

BC2—7/78

Please allow four weeks for delivery. This offer expires 1/79.

Barbara Cartland's Library of Love

The World's Great Stories of Romance Specially Abridged by Barbara Cartland For Today's Readers.